HANNAH MONTANA

ROCK THE WAVES

by Suzanne Harper

Based on the series created by Michael Poryes and Rich Correll & Barry O'Brien

Disney Press
New York

ROCK THE WAVES

For Hannah (and Miley!)
fans everywhere.

Printed in the United States of America
First Edition
1 3 5 7 9 10 8 6 4 2

Library of Congress Cataloging-in-Publication Data on file.
ISBN 978-1-4231-1181-8

For more Disney Press fun, visit www.disneybooks.com
Visit DisneyChannel.com

Reinforced binding

Designed by Roberta Pressel

Chapter One

Ride the wave
Summer sun, summer fun, summer love
Ride the wave
Let it bring you what you're dreaming of

The sun had already risen high in the cloudless blue sky over Malibu by the time fifteen-year-old Miley Stewart woke up. She pushed a strand of brown hair out of her eyes and blinked sleepily at her bedroom ceiling, sensing that there was something different—something delightful—about this morning. The only problem was that she couldn't quite remember what it was.

Two birds sang sweetly to each other in the jacaranda tree outside. She turned her head toward the window, smiling, then realized that this was the first thing that was different: she could actually *hear* the birds. Usually, the gentle sound of birdsong would be totally drowned out by the painful sound of her older brother, Jackson, singing loudly and incredibly off-key in the bathroom.

She lay still for another moment, luxuriating in the sense of peace and watching dust motes dance lazily in the sunlight that slanted through the window curtains.

Then she stretched her arms over her head, enjoying the feeling of being completely rested and relaxed . . . which, now that she thought about it, was also strange. Usually, every morning started with her desperately trying to find the braying alarm clock so she could hit the snooze button one more time—

That was it! Her alarm clock hadn't gone off! Miley bolted out of bed, panicky, and raced to her closet. She should have known as soon as she saw the way the sunbeams crossed her room that the sun was higher in the sky than usual, which meant that it was very late, which meant that she would probably miss the first bell, which meant—

She stopped abruptly in the middle of the room as she finally remembered the glorious fact that had been nagging at her since she first woke up.

No, she wasn't going to be tardy. Because *this* was the first day of summer! Three months of fun and friends and freedom stretched out in front of her, like a glorious present waiting to be unwrapped!

Miley did a little dance of joy before running out of her room and down the stairs.

"Good morning!" she called out to her father, who was mixing pancake batter in the kitchen.

"Well, someone's in a good mood today," Robby Stewart said teasingly. "Hmm. I wonder why that is?"

"Because I'm free," she said happily. "Free, free, free!"

Miley skidded to a stop and reached over the counter to put a finger in the bowl of batter. "Free," she repeated dreamily one more time as she licked her finger.

"Whoa, there, bud, you can lick the bowl *after* I've finished making pancakes for everybody," her father said.

"But there won't *be* any batter left after you've made the pancakes," Miley pointed out reasonably. She snuck her finger in the bowl again. "Yum."

"Mornin'." Jackson, Miley's brother, wandered into the kitchen. His tousled dark-blond hair made it clear he'd just stumbled out of bed. So did the fact that he was still wearing pajama bottoms and a T-shirt. Yawning, he grabbed a plate and held it out to his dad. "The pancakes smell great. I'll have five, please. No, seven. Actually, I'm starving, so how about eight. . . ."

"Whoa, whoa, whoa," Mr. Stewart said. "Don't you want to take a gander at my works of art here first?"

Miley rolled her eyes. Her father had grown very proud of his ability to create what he called "picture pancakes"—batter poured to resemble objects and animals—and insisted on asking his children to identify them before being served.

Unfortunately, trying to figure out what the pancakes were supposed to be wasn't always that easy. Mr. Stewart would claim that the pancakes were alien spacecraft or giraffes or pickup trucks, but they all looked like blobs to Miley. Tasty blobs, but blobs nonetheless.

Jackson peered suspiciously at the skillet. "Oh, man. Is that a tarantula? You know I hate eating anything that looks like a spider."

"Now, why in tarnation would I make a tarantula pancake?" his father asked testily. "Look closer."

Jackson tried again. "An octopus?"

"No! Open your eyes, boy!"

Jackson's stomach growled. His hunger drove him to start making wild guesses. "An amoeba? A sailing ship? A car engine?"

"No, no, and no." His father flipped the pancake, looking hurt. "It's a palm tree! I can't believe you couldn't see that!"

"Oh, yeah, *now* I do," Jackson said, hoping to get back in his dad's good graces—and get some breakfast—as soon as possible. "I must not be awake yet! Or maybe that gnawing hunger in my stomach is making me so light-headed that I can't think properly." He held out his plate with a hopeful expression.

"Nice try," Mr. Stewart said grumpily, but he slid a few pancakes onto his son's plate. As he was adding a touch of nutmeg to the batter, the back door opened and Lilly Truscott, Miley's best friend, burst into the room carrying a Boogie board. She was wearing a T-shirt and shorts over her bathing suit, and her blond hair was braided in a no-nonsense way that meant she was ready for action. "Hey, everybody! Happy first day of summer vacation!"

She traded a high-five with Miley, then

sniffed the air. "Wow, something sure smells delicious."

Mr. Stewart beamed as he carefully poured more batter in the skillet. "That would be my world-famous pancakes," he bragged. "Come on, Lilly. Check out this one."

Lilly gave Miley a long-suffering look; she had been subjected to picture pancakes on several occasions when she had slept over at the Stewarts' house.

"Daddy, just let us eat breakfast!" Miley cried. "We're so hungry!"

"In a second, bud," he said. "Take a gander at this skillet, Lilly. You're usually good at this."

Reluctantly, Lilly went over to the stove. "Um, is it, maybe, a . . . snowman?"

"A snowman?" Mr. Stewart asked, outraged. "Snowmen are for amateurs. I moved past snowmen years ago!"

"A rose garden? A map of the United States? A line of ducks walking through a puddle?" Under pressure, Lilly was beginning to babble as much as Jackson had.

Exasperated, Mr. Stewart held out the skillet to the room and pointed at the pancake with his spatula. "It's Mount Rushmore!" he said, as if this were blindingly obvious. "Can't you see how I used extra cinnamon on Lincoln's beard?"

Miley, Lilly, and Jackson stared at the pancake doubtfully.

"Come on," Mr. Stewart said. "Just squint your left eye and tilt your head to the right and you'll see it plain as the nose on your face."

"Oh. Yeah. Of course," Miley said, trying not to laugh. "I *can't* believe I didn't see that from the beginning."

"I think I need to take you kids to the eye doctor," her father said grumpily as he started a new batch of pancakes. "You're developing serious vision problems."

The door opened again and Oliver Oken, Miley's other best friend, bounded into the kitchen, smiling. *"Hola!"* he cried. He had started taking Spanish and liked to use his newfound vocabulary whenever possible. *"Cómo estás?"*

"Hey, Oliver," Miley said. *"Bueno."*

"Hi, Miley," he said. "Morning, Mr. Stewart." He peered into the pan, brushing his brown bangs out of his eyes so that he could get a better look. "That's an airplane, isn't it?" he asked. "A 747 jumbo jet, if I'm not mistaken?"

Mr. Stewart brightened immediately. "Got it first time out of the chute!" he cried before turning an accusing glare on the others. "See what happens when people take artistic creation seriously?" He turned back to Oliver. "You feel like breakfast, Oliver?"

"You bet." Oliver's brown eyes lit up. True, he had just finished eating two bowls of cereal and four pieces of toast, but he reasoned that he needed extra nutrition because he was still growing. At least, he *hoped* he was still growing.

"Then grab a seat." Mr. Stewart put a plate

with a stack of pancakes on the breakfast table. "And get to eatin', everybody. The pancakes may be pretty as a picture, but they aren't any good when they're cold."

"Thanks!" Oliver speared a few pancakes, poured on some syrup, and dug in. "So, Miley, what's so important we had to get up at the crack of dawn on our very first day of summer vacation?"

"*That's* what's important," she said. "Vacation! I counted up last night. We only have one hundred days of freedom! We have to make the most of it. So I have called you here today for a summer-strategy session—"

"You sound like you're running for president," Jackson mumbled through a big bite of pancake.

"And you sound like you're talking with your mouth full," she snapped back.

"Hey, be sweet, you two," their father said. "No fussin' or feudin' over the flapjacks! Especially not flapjacks like these—flapjacks that belong in a museum." He took one last appreciative look at his own plate. "That's Elvis," he said, pointing to his breakfast before taking a bite.

"First," Miley went on, thinking out loud, "we have to be sure to block out mornings at the beach."

"Absolutely. That's a given," Lilly said. She gave her friend an encouraging look. "Maybe this will be the summer you'll finally let me teach you how to surf."

But Miley shook her head. "No way," she said with finality. "You *know* I'd be taking my life in my hands."

Lilly was a total athlete. She loved skateboarding, surfing, running, playing basketball. But even though Miley had grown up riding horses on a farm in Tennessee, she was a major klutz when it came to most sports. She was always the last one picked for the team in gym class, the first one to drop a ball or twist an ankle. The thought of trying to balance on a surfboard while also braving the crashing waves of Malibu made her break out in a nervous sweat. So, as much as Lilly begged her to give surfing a go, Miley had always managed to resist.

"You'd love it if you just gave it a try," Lilly wheedled. "And we'd have even more time to hang out once you learned. Just think about it."

"Okay." Miley put her finger to her chin and frowned to demonstrate how hard she was thinking. Then she shook her head again. "The answer's still no."

Lilly sighed. "Well, at least we can hang out at the park. They've got a sweet new half-pipe."

Miley had silently resolved never to try skateboarding, either, but she decided this was not the best time to mention that. Instead, she tried a diversionary tactic. "We also have to make time for shopping," she said.

Her tactic worked. Lilly's face brightened. Here was an activity they could both whole-heartedly enjoy. "Summer sales at the mall are a must," she agreed.

Oliver looked up from his pancakes in alarm. Once shopping entered the summer-planning discussion, he knew it was time to make his opinion heard. "Don't forget going to the movies," he said. "'Tis the season of summer blockbusters!"

"Yeah," Miley said. "See what I mean? There's so much to do!" Her eyes narrowed in thought. "Maybe we should try and make a schedule—"

"Whoa, bud, slow down there!" Mr. Stewart said. "I hate to be the one to break it to you, Miley, but this summer isn't going to be all fun and games."

"It isn't?" Miley eyed her dad warily. "Why not?"

He eyed her back. "Well, I've got some good news and some bad news. Which do you want first?"

Miley bit her lip. She hated these kinds of choices; they made her feel like her life had become a game show, she had just entered the crucial final round, and she was about to give a completely wrong answer.

As she hesitated, Oliver jumped in with his advice. "Ask for the bad news first. That way, you get the worst over with right away. It's like tearing off a Band-Aid—if you do it fast, it doesn't hurt."

Lilly rolled her eyes. "The last time you took off a Band-Aid, you screamed so loud your mom called 911," she said. She turned to Miley. "Ask for the good news first. Then you'll already be happy when you hear the bad news. It will soften the blow."

"How about no news and we all get to go back to bed?" Jackson grumbled, spearing another pancake.

"What'll it be, bud?" Mr. Stewart asked. "Your call."

"Bad news . . . no, wait, wait!" Miley squeezed her eyes tight, crossed her fingers, and finally blurted out: "Good news! I want the good news first!"

"Okay," her dad said. "Here goes. The Breakpoint Surf Series is coming to Malibu—"

"The Breakpoint Surf Series?" Lilly jumped to her feet, her eyes sparkling with excitement. "Miley, that's fantastic! Fantastic, stupendous, *awesome* good news! Why, you ask?"

"Okay," Miley said agreeably. "Why?"

"Because the top competitor in the Breakpoint Surf Series is none other than"—Lilly paused before yelling the last two words—"Talen Wright!"

"Talen Wright?" Miley yelled back. "No!"

"Yes!"

"No!"

"Yes!"

She and Lilly started jumping up and down, squealing with delight. After a few moments, Miley realized that her father, Jackson, and Oliver were all staring at them in complete bewilderment.

"Who in tarnation are you girls talking about?" her dad asked.

"Talen Wright!" Miley explained.

Still nothing but blank faces. Miley spared one pitying glance for their ignorance and set out to enlighten them. "He's this Australian guy—"

"Who happens to be one of the top surfers in the world!" Lilly interrupted, too excited to be quiet.

"Even though he's only sixteen!" Miley rushed on. "Plus, he's totally—"

"—totally—" Lilly said.

"—cute!" they finished together.

Then they looked at each other and squealed again.

"Huh." Mr. Stewart didn't look convinced. "Sounds more like he's totally, totally trouble to me."

But Miley wasn't listening. She had developed a major crush on Talen a few months ago when he was chosen as the cover for *Teen Talk* magazine's Gorgeous Guys issue. She had instantly subscribed to *Teen Talk* to make sure she got the latest Talen Wright news; she had started watching surfing competitions on TV; she had daydreamed constantly about meeting him. And now, he was coming to Malibu!

"Talen Wright," she murmured to herself. Even his name sounded cute.

Oliver scowled and took an extralarge bite of pancake. "What kind of name is Talen, anyway?" he muttered.

But Miley didn't hear him because her father was trying to get back to his main point. "As I was saying," he went on, "the good news is, there's going to be a big concert in two weeks at the end of the surfing contest. And the organizers want Hannah Montana to be the headliner!"

Miley and Lilly just stared at him, too stunned to speak.

What both Lilly and Oliver knew, and most of the world did not, was that Miley Stewart was not a typical high school student. She had a secret identity as Hannah Montana, one of the biggest pop stars in the world. Sometimes Miley had a hard time juggling her two lives, but most of the time she felt, as her hit song was called, that she had "The Best of Both Worlds."

Like, for example, right now.

Lilly found her voice first. "Miley," she whispered. "You are so, so lucky."

"I know." Miley nodded, her eyes wide.

"If you give a concert for the surf series, you could actually get to meet Talen Wright." Lilly held out her arm. "Look! I have goosebumps!"

"Me too!" Miley said, holding out her own arm.

Oliver pushed his empty plate away. He had been thinking about having another pancake or two, but somehow he wasn't that hungry anymore. "Big deal. So you're going to meet some sunburned surfer dude. I bet he uses words like 'gnarly' and 'cowabunga.' I bet he tells people he's 'stoked.'"

"Who cares about his conversation?" Lilly sighed, a faraway look in her eyes.

"Who cares if he can even talk," Miley agreed.

Her dad cleared his throat meaningfully. Miley's smile dimmed. She didn't know anyone else who could clear his throat in such an ominous way.

"Okay," she said. "The good news is way too good to be true. So, lay it on me. What's the bad news?"

"I had a talk with your principal last week. It seems you got a little behind in your schoolwork from going on the road for those concerts last winter. Specifically, you got a little behind in English class." He gave her a serious look. "Apparently, you were supposed to keep a journal all semester. Ring a bell?"

"Oh, right." Miley's toes curled guiltily. Of course she had *meant* to keep up with her journal, but somehow all the rehearsals and costume fittings and talk show appearances kept getting in the way. And then she had started putting off one assignment with the idea that she would double up the next week, and before long she had fallen so far behind that she had stopped even thinking about the class because it made her so anxious. She shuddered just thinking about it. "Maybe just a *little*."

"Uh-huh."

"But the teacher didn't take off many points!" she went on quickly. "I just got a B instead of a B plus. That's still a very decent grade—most parents would be proud."

But her father shook his head. "We talked about this before your last tour, Miley," he said. "I'm willing to let you miss a few days of school here and there if you keep up with *all* your homework. But I don't want you to get used to taking shortcuts, even if your grades are still okay."

Miley bit her lip. "I know, I know," she

said. "I'll do better next year, I promise."

"Actually," Mr. Stewart said, "you'll do better *this* year. Turns out your principal came up with a way for you to make up that work."

"Really?" Miley brightened a bit at this news. "So, what, I just have to write an essay or something?"

Jackson snorted. "Poor, dear, sweet Miley. How little you know of principals' evil ways. They're fiendish, they're cunning, they're—"

"Willing to give you a second chance," his father interrupted, with a stern glance at his son. "There's a summer school class for students who need to bring up their English grades. You'll be attending a special two-hour tutoring session every day for the next two weeks with Mr. Dickson."

"What? No! Not every day! Not two hours! No!" Miley felt as if she'd been in the middle of a beautiful dream, only to be awakened by a pail of freezing water dumped over her head. "That will ruin my entire summer!"

"Gee, that's too bad, Miley," Jackson said. He added pompously, "But I think it's about time you realized that actions have consequences, don't you?" He stretched his arms over his head with satisfaction. "Now I, on the other hand, am free as a bird. Yep, this summer, I'm going to be hanging out at the beach, soaking up the sun, and meeting beautiful surfer girls. Life doesn't get any sweeter than that!"

Jackson jumped up from the table and started moving in what Miley supposed was a victory dance, although she privately thought it looked more like he was trying to get a bug out from underneath his shirt.

His father coughed and Jackson froze midtwist. "What?" he asked apprehensively. His father's cough was just as bad as his throat-clearing. Nothing good ever followed it.

"I also had a little chat with Rico's dad," Mr. Stewart said. "Seems like summer is a real busy time at the surf shop, so he'd love to have

have you work a double shift for the next month. Which will also help you pay for that fender bender you had with my car."

"What? No! Double shifts? For the next month? No!" Jackson said.

"Wow," Oliver said. "That's brutal."

Lilly rolled her eyes. "How hard can it be to make smoothies and hand people bottles of water?" she asked. "We're not talking rocket science here."

"Sure, it *looks* easy," Jackson said huffily. "The good ones always make it look easy." He flopped back down in his chair and gave his father an accusing look. "My summer is ruined. I'm going to waste my time slaving over a smoothie machine, just because I had one teensy-weensy accident—"

"Which destroyed my car's bumper," his dad pointed out.

Jackson's mouth fell open at this outrageous claim. "Destroyed? It was only dented!" he shouted. "In fact, it wasn't even a real dent.

More like an itty-bitty, teeny-tiny, practically invisible ding!"

"Which cost five hundred dollars," his dad said.

Jackson threw himself back into his chair and crossed his arms sulkily. "I should just open a body shop," he muttered. "I could be a millionaire by the time I'm twenty-five."

"Look at it this way, Jackson," Miley said sweetly. "This experience will help you learn that actions have consequences, won't it?"

He shot her a poisonous glare. "At least *my* job is at the beach," he said. "But don't worry, I'll be sure to think of you, stuck in a boring classroom for hours, staring out the window, wishing you could trade places with me for just one measly minute—"

"Okay, kids, remember, you'll still have time for lots of fun this summer," Mr. Stewart interrupted hastily. "You just have to work a little bit, too."

Miley sighed as her dream of three whole

months of freedom vanished before her eyes. "But *summer school*," she said mournfully.

Then Lilly caught her eye and mouthed the words, "Talen Wright."

Miley smiled, slightly more cheerful.

Lilly mouthed two more words, "Hannah Montana."

Immediately, Miley's spirits lifted even higher. After all, she loved performing more than anything in the world—and what could be better than doing a concert in Malibu, practically her own backyard? Plus, even if she never got to meet Talen Wright, for a few brief, shining moments, they would both be breathing the same air.

That alone would make this summer golden.

Chapter Two

First I saw your laughing eyes
Blue as the sea, blue as the skies

The only good thing about summer school, Miley thought, was that it didn't start until ten o'clock, so she could sleep in a bit. She should be grateful for that, at least.

As she walked toward the school's main entrance, she caught a glimpse of her reflection in a window. Hair pulled back in a scraggly ponytail, faded T-shirt and shorts, flip-flops . . .

She should be also grateful that she felt absolutely no pressure about her appearance, since she seriously doubted that she would want to attract the attention of her fellow detainees.

And, oh, yeah—she also should be grateful for being given a chance to raise her English grade. At least, that's what her father had said to her a minimum of five times this morning before she had set off.

But as Miley trudged up the sidewalk to Seaview High School, she wasn't in a grateful mood. She paused outside the main door and scowled up at the building.

"Stupid, stupid summer school," she muttered. Then she pushed the door open and walked to room 217, where she was to be imprisoned. As she entered the classroom, her eyes flicked around the room to see who her fellow inmates were.

Dan Barton, of course. Jackie Somers, naturally. Eugene Fields, to be expected. How had she managed to end up sentenced to two long weeks with the school's most notorious slackers?

"Good morning, Miley," the teacher, Mr. Dickson, said. "Glad you could join us.

Perhaps the second time will be the charm, and you'll find a way to finish *all* your assignments."

Oh, right. *That* was how she had ended up here.

"We're just waiting for a few more students, then we'll be ready to get started," Mr. Dickson said. Even though it was summer, the teacher wore pressed gray pants, a white shirt buttoned to the collar, and black dress shoes.

Miley sighed and headed for a desk near the window. At least she could glance outside occasionally and remember what freedom looked like. She gazed wistfully at the clear blue sky, the golden sunshine, the shimmer of the ocean in the distance.

Hmm. Maybe it would be better to move to the back corner, where she wouldn't be mocked by the beautiful summer day outside. . . .

The door opened. She glanced up. Her mouth dropped open in shock, and she stopped thinking about where she should sit. All her attention was focused on the boy who stood framed in the doorway. He had wavy blond hair, blue eyes, and a dazzling smile; he was wearing faded shorts and a T-shirt with a picture of a kangaroo riding a surfboard; he had an athletic build, and he looked exactly like . . .

"Talen Wright?" Mr. Dickson asked, looking up from his attendance sheet.

"Yeah, g'day," the boy said. "I guess this is the right place, if I'm on your list?"

"Indeed it is," the teacher replied. Talen was followed into the room by a very pretty girl with three earrings in each ear and long blonde hair streaked with blue, green, and purple highlights. A boy with a wild mop of red hair and a resigned expression trailed into the room after her.

Mr. Dickson said, "I'd like to welcome our surfing contingent, Talen Wright, Jessica Stirling, and Stefan Oblonsky. Say hello, everyone."

Amid a chorus of mumbled hellos, Miley sat silent. She felt as if she were in a dream. To be more precise, she felt as if she were still in the dream she had had last night, in which Talen Wright had taken a starring role.

But this clearly wasn't a dream.

In fact, he was sitting down next to her!

He turned his head. "Hi."

Now he was saying hi to her!

"My name's Talen."

And he was telling her his name!

He gave her a puzzled look, and she realized she still hadn't managed to say anything in response. "Oh, hi, my name is Miley, nice to meet you," she said quickly, her words almost running together.

He grinned. "Same here. Just sorry we had to meet under these circumstances."

"Under these?" For a second, Miley was confused. "Oh, right! You mean in summer school!"

Jessica, the surfer with the multicolored hair, had nabbed the desk in front of Talen.

Now she turned around and gave Miley an amused glance. "Exactly. Here in summer school. Where we don't want to be," she said in a slow, careful voice, as if explaining something to a child.

Miley blushed. Jessica had an Australian accent, just like Talen, but somehow her voice didn't sound warm or charming or endearing at all.

"Well, why *are* you here?" she blurted out. Jessica lifted one cool eyebrow, and Miley felt even more flustered. "I mean, the rest of us all have to make up some assignments from English class, but you don't even go to this school."

"Dude, we've been, like, chasing waves around the world for six months!" Stefan leaned over from his spot on the other side of Talen. "It's, like, seriously hard to study."

"The organizers try to find ways to keep us hitting the books and to help us make up work," Talen added. "So here we are."

"Of course, it's *completely* boring," Jessica

chimed in. She twirled one long lock of hair—a lime-green section, Miley noticed—between her fingers. "But that's the price we have to pay for being on the professional surfing circuit, right, Talen?"

"Um, yeah," he said, not looking at her. "Right."

"Everyone always thinks that being a pro surfer is so exciting," Jessica confided to Miley. "Just because we travel the world, and we're on TV all the time, and people want our autographs, and magazines beg us to do photo shoots. But you know, being a celebrity is actually *very* hard work."

"Oh, really," Miley said, hiding a smile. If only Jessica knew that she was lecturing Hannah Montana about the ups and downs of celebrity life! "I guess I never thought of that. How hard it is, I mean."

"Yes, it's not quite as glamorous as it looks to outsiders," she went on. From her superior tone of voice, Miley knew exactly what Jessica meant by "outsiders." She meant "people who aren't famous." She meant "people who don't count." She meant "people like *you*."

Miley no longer felt any urge to smile. "Well, it's too bad you have to be stuck in a classroom when you could be surfing," she said as politely as she could.

Talen stretched his legs out into the aisle. "Oh, I don't know about that," he said, smiling at her. "Things could be a lot worse."

Miley looked at Talen uncertainly. Was he actually flirting with her?

Out of the corner of her eye, Miley saw Jessica turn around to face the front of the room, clearly disgruntled. Talen saw it too, and gave Miley a conspiratorial wink.

He was! He was flirting with her!

She secretly moved her left hand down and gave her leg a pinch.

Ouch. Yep, she was awake.

"Yeah," she said, smiling back. "Things could definitely be worse."

"What do I like to do more than anything else in the world?" Dan Barton slowly repeated the question, which had been posed by Mr. Dickson in a futile attempt to start a lively class discussion—or *any* class discussion.

Mr. Dickson had begun the class by informing them that their daily assignment would be to write in a journal about a subject that was important to them. As the days went on, they would be revising their entries which they would turn in at the end of the session to be graded.

"In order to write well, you should choose a subject that means something to you," he had explained. "So that's what I'd like you to do. Write about whatever you want, as long as it's something you really care about."

Then he had suggested that they share a few topic ideas with each other, which had led directly to the painful experience that Miley was now enduring.

"Hmm," Dan went on. "That's an *extremely* hard question, Mr. Dickson. I'll have to give that some serious thought."

He is clearly playing dumb just to exasperate our teacher, Miley thought. And, from the looks of the vein that was throbbing in Mr. Dickson's forehead, it's working.

"Maybe there's a sport you enjoy playing?" Mr. Dickson suggested with little hope in his voice. "Or a hobby you've picked up?"

"No, nothing comes to mind," he said, sounding even more befuddled. "Nothing . . . at . . . all." Dan squinted up at the ceiling, as if hoping to find the answer written there, then shook his head.

Miley bit her lip to keep from suggesting a topic for him. Dan Barton had been in one of her classes last year, so she knew for a fact that he liked flicking spitballs at anyone who sat within ten feet of him. He liked that *a lot*.

Mr. Dickson rubbed his eyes wearily. "Come on now. The field is wide open here."

"Oh!" Dan sat up straight, as if suddenly struck by inspiration. Mr. Dickson looked encouraged until Dan said, "Does sleeping count? Because I recently started getting into recreational napping, and I think if I do well as an amateur I might have a chance to go pro—"

Miley resisted the urge to let her head drop to her desk in despair.

From across the aisle, Talen caught her eye and smiled, as if he knew exactly how she was feeling. Miley grinned back.

"No, Mr. Barton," Mr. Dickson said, his jaw starting to clench. "Sleeping does not count. Anyone else?" When no hands went up, he sighed and said, "Okay, let me pick a volunteer. How about you, Talen?"

To Miley's surprise, Talen seemed flustered. He looked down and shuffled his feet. Finally he muttered, "Well, I like surfing, of course. . . ."

His voice trailed off, leaving silence in its wake.

"Good, good." Mr. Dickson seemed happy

to get any kind of response, even one as luke-warm as Talen's. "So, can you elaborate on that a bit? The more you talk about your ideas now, the further ahead you'll be when you have to sit down and face that dreaded blank page, right?"

Talen slid down in his chair. "Right," he murmured. "Well . . . I guess it's because I grew up near the ocean. . . ."

His voice drifted off again. Jessica jumped in to fill the silence. "I know what I'll write about!" she cried. "I like competing. Being on tour. Being the *best*. Of course, it was hard to work up the nerve to enter my first competi-tion—"

Really? Miley thought. Because you sure as shootin' don't seem like the shy, retiring type to me.

"—but now here I am, one of the top women surfers in the world," Jessica went on modestly. "Koala Kool Sportswear just signed me as their spokesmodel. I'm going to be on the cover of *Surfing Illustrated* next month.

And my agent is in talks with a production company in Los Angeles—they want to make a reality show about the Breakpoint Surf Series!"

She finally stopped to take a breath, and not a moment too soon, Miley thought.

"Well, you certainly do have a lot of material to work with," Mr. Dickson said, a little taken aback by this rush of information. "Now, does anyone else want to share their topic with the class before we finish up—"

"Of course, everyone on the tour will be in the TV show, not just me," Jessica added. "But my agent says there's always one breakout person on every reality show who becomes a big star, and he thinks my chances are good."

"Yes, indeed," Mr. Dickson said. "Quite exciting for you. Anyone else—"

"Actually, he said my chances are very good," Jessica corrected herself. "Not just good. *Very* good."

"Please remember to include that," the teacher said dryly. "I'm sure it will add a whole new dimension to your essay. Miley, we haven't heard from you. We only have a few more minutes, but do you want to talk a bit about your topic?"

"Oh, well, that's easy," Miley said. "What I love more than anything else in the world is music."

"Ah. And why is that?"

She opened her mouth to answer Mr. Dickson and suddenly had an inkling about why Talen had had such a hard time answering this seemingly simple question.

Of course she loved music; it was her whole life. And that was the problem. How could she possibly talk about something that important, that secret, and that personal to a roomful of people, some of them strangers and some of them—she caught a glimpse of Eugene picking his nose and quickly looked away—well, some of them, frankly, just a little freaky.

Miley didn't have the right words to

explain why she loved music. And the words she did have would sound too . . . *drippy*. Her cheeks burned with embarrassment at the very thought of saying them out loud.

"Um, well, I just do," she finished lamely.

"Okay, that's a good starting point," Mr. Dickson said, trying to stay positive. "Well, I hope that tonight's assignment will help all of you develop your feelings about your topic in a bit more detail. I suggest you start by writing about the first time you remember becoming fascinated with music—or with surfing, Talen, or napping, Dan, if you absolutely can't think of anything else. Let that memory come to the surface and write down whatever comes to mind, any thought that pops into your head. And now—" Mr. Dickson looked at his watch and gave a sigh of relief. "I'll see you all in the morning."

As the equally relieved students spilled out into the hall, Miley found herself walking beside Talen.

"I'm going to do some surfing this afternoon, try to get a feel for the waves," he said. "If you're not doing anything, do you want to go to the beach with me?"

Yes, yes, a thousand times yes! Miley thought.

Jessica walked by just in time to hear this. "New town, new crush," she said in a snide tone. "Right, Talen?"

Before he could answer, she breezed on past them and headed for the door.

Talen rolled his eyes. "Don't mind her," he said. "She's completely mad."

Miley looked after Jessica, who pushed the front door open with unnecessary force and stomped out into the sunshine. "I'll say she is. Why is she so angry?"

For a moment he looked puzzled, then his face cleared and he laughed. "No, not mad as in angry," he explained. "Back in Oz, mad means crazy. As in mental, loony, off her gourd. No worries, though, she can't harm you as long as I'm around."

Miley felt a flutter in her stomach and tried desperately to think of a witty rejoinder. Unfortunately, the only thing that popped into her mind—I can't wait to tell Lilly about this!—was neither witty nor appropriate.

Fortunately, Talen kept talking. "So, what do you say? Want to head for the beach?"

"Sure, I'd love to," she said, trying to sound cool. "Maybe we could meet up with my friend Lilly. She loves to surf. I know she'd love meeting you."

Okay, stop talking now, Miley, she thought. Or at least stop using the word "love" before Talen gets the wrong idea. Or, actually, the right idea. Although, come to think of it, you also don't want him to get the right idea, because that would mean he would know that you had a huge, huge crush on him—

Before she could get herself any more confused, she added, "Lilly's probably hanging out at Rico's. We could grab a snack, too."

"Awesome," he said. "Let's go."

๑จ๕ *Chapter Three*

Hit me like a wave that summer day
Told me come along and play

Rico's was an open-air snack shop on the beach, decorated in a summer-surf-and-sand theme. When Miley and Talen showed up, Jackson was working behind the counter, while Lilly and Oliver sat at a table drinking sodas.

Miley had to give Lilly credit. When she introduced Talen, Jackson and Oliver took it in stride, but for a brief moment, Miley thought Lilly might faint.

But Lilly was made of sterner stuff than that. She recovered almost instantly and even managed to act completely composed as she shook his hand.

True, when Talen turned his back on her to check out the smoothie specials, Lilly started waving her arms wildly at Miley, apparently trying to send some kind of message through a combination of mime and hand signals.

Miley couldn't make out the actual words, but she had a pretty good idea of what Lilly's message was, since the experience of meeting Talen was so fresh in her own mind. Something along the lines of, Oh, my gosh, I can't believe it's him and he's standing right here in front of me, oh, my gosh, oh, my gosh, this is so cool! That would be Miley's guess, anyway.

"Lilly," she said out of the corner of her mouth. "Chill."

When Talen turned around to say, "Do you guys want anything to drink?" Lilly immediately dropped her arms and leaned casually on her surfboard, the picture of nonchalance.

"No thanks, Talen," she said. "I'm about to hit the waves. Don't want anything weighing me down."

"Miley told me you surf. Very cool."

Lilly blushed with pleasure. "Yeah, I've been doing it for a few years," she said casually.

"And she's great," Miley added. "A real natural."

"I don't know about that," Lilly said, blushing even more. "I wish I could do some of the tricks you do, Talen. The way you won your last competition by coming from behind in the last round? That was sweet."

"Thanks, but all it takes is practice," he said. "You know, if you've been surfing for that long, you should think about entering the competition here in Malibu."

Miley saw a look of mingled excitement and fear cross Lilly's face. "Really? That would be awesome! But, no, I couldn't, not really—"

"Sure you could," he said encouragingly. "There's a novice section for people who haven't competed before. You could try it out, see how you like it. That's how I started."

"You really think I could hold my own?" Lilly asked.

"You'll never know unless you try," he pointed out. "If you want, I can introduce you to some of the organizers. They'll get you signed up."

"That would be amazing!" Lilly's face was glowing. "Thanks."

"No worries." Talen turned to Miley. "I've got to get some practice in, but maybe we could get together tomorrow after class and work on our journal entries?"

She beamed. "Sure, that sounds great."

"Cool. See you tomorrow." He sketched a small salute in Jackson and Oliver's direction and headed across the sand toward the water.

When he was a safe distance away, Lilly turned and gave Miley a huge, excited grin. "Talen Wright!" she whispered.

"I know!" Miley whispered back.

"Well, I don't see what the big deal about Talen Wright is," Jackson grumbled. "He's just another guy who happens to have an Australian accent."

"An *adorable* Australian accent," Miley corrected him in a dreamy voice.

Oliver asked, "Is that all it takes to make the girls go—"

He caught Jackson's eye and together they started jumping up and down, squealing, "Talen! Talen! Talen!"

"Don't be so silly," Miley said with great dignity.

"We're just acting the way you and Lilly were yesterday," her brother shot back. Then he paused, as if replaying that comment in his mind. "Oh. You're right. We *were* being silly."

"I meant, don't be silly enough to think that all it takes is an accent," she snapped. "He also happens to be an athlete who has remained modest despite the many major competitions he has won around the world and despite his cover-worthy looks, which include sun-bleached hair, sapphire blue eyes, and a perfect tan."

Jackson and Oliver stared at her.

"What?" she asked defensively. "I'm just quoting what *Teen Talk* said about him!"

"*Teen Talk*! Please." Jackson rolled his eyes. "No guy is that perfect. Believe me."

"Talen is," Lilly said, loyally coming to Miley's aid. "Did you know that his astrological sign is Pisces, which is a water sign, which explains why he's so good at surfing?"

"Or that his favorite color is turquoise blue," Miley added, "which is the color of the ocean in Fiji, which happens to be number one on his list of top-ten favorite places in the world?"

"Or that his favorite book is *The Old Man and the Sea*?" Lilly said. "Or"—a look of sheer bliss crossed her face—"that he's going to help me enter my first surfing competition!"

Her eyes met Miley's. They screamed in unison.

"Oh!" A sudden, nerve-racking thought struck Lilly. "I really should get in a couple more sets before it gets dark. And then I need to wax up my surfboard. And I definitely have to go to the mall and buy a much cuter bathing suit—"

She grabbed her surfboard and headed for the water. Before she could take three steps, however, Oliver blocked her way.

"I thought you were finished surfing for the day," he complained. "I thought we were going to the movies."

"Maybe tomorrow," Lilly said, trying to step around him.

But Oliver moved to get in front of her again. "I thought you couldn't wait to see *Sk8ter Summer*," he said accusingly. "I thought we agreed that we would see it together."

"The movie will still be playing next week," Lilly said.

"But this is opening night!" Oliver insisted. "I marked it on my calendar."

Lilly glared at him. "Plans change, okay? We have the whole summer to go to the movies, but the Breakpoint Surf Series is in only two weeks! That means I only have two weeks to practice and prepare. I can't waste a moment!"

"Okay, okay, fine," Oliver said, giving up. "Tell you what, we'll save *Sk8ter Summer* for later, when you can go." He turned to give Miley a beseeching look. "But tonight . . . Miley, what do you want to see? How about *Night of the Zombie Bats*? The trailer looks pretty awesome."

Miley bit her lip and exchanged a wild glance with Lilly. "Oh, thanks, Oliver, but I'm going to be busy tonight, too."

His face fell. "Doing what?"

Doing what? Behind his back, Lilly was grimacing in sympathy. Miley would never have to tell *Lilly* that she had to go right home and start planning the outfit she would wear to summer school tomorrow. That would be painfully obvious to another girl; it wouldn't even be worth explaining.

But not only would Oliver not understand

why she had to spend any time figuring out her clothes, he would be completely baffled by why it would take at least three hours.

"Um, I have a lot of homework," she said, thinking fast.

Oliver's eyes narrowed with suspicion. "Already?"

"Oh, yeah." She nodded vigorously. "Man, summer school! It's a killer! But tomorrow we'll do something for sure, okay?"

Oliver still looked disappointed, but he said, "Okay."

"Great." She gave him a big smile. "See you later!"

Then she went off to check out her closet and reread her entire stack of *Teen Talk* magazines in preparation for class the next day.

Chapter Four

You took my hand and said let's go
I'll teach you a whole new show

Summer vacation was only a few days old, and Oliver was already feeling bored, grumpy, and very, very lonely. He called Lilly right after breakfast to see if she wanted to hang out until Miley got out of school, but Lilly brushed him off.

"I can't, Oliver, I have to do a conditioning run this morning," she said.

"But it's summer," he pleaded. "A time to *chill* out, not *work* out!"

Even over his cell phone, which did not have the best reception, he sensed Lilly's impatience. "I'm entering my very first surfing competition, Oliver," she snapped. "And Talen said he runs five miles a day, so I'm going to do the same thing."

"I should have known Talen was behind this," Oliver grumbled. "What am I supposed to do while Miley's in school and you're on the beach getting heatstroke?"

He knew he sounded a little whiny, but he didn't care. Only two days ago, the three of them had been making plans for everything they were going to do this summer. And now, here he was, sitting at home with only his video game system to keep him company.

"You could always come with," Lilly offered. "It wouldn't hurt you to get a little exercise, you know. That last gym class was pretty sad."

Oliver held his cell phone away from his face and stared at it for a moment in disbelief. Then he put it back to his ear and said, "Hey, if I hadn't been completely worn out from studying for finals, I would have definitely been able to run around the track ten times. Twenty times, even!"

"You keeled over halfway through the first lap," Lilly reminded him. "And the coach had to help you off the field."

"Thank you, Lilly," Oliver said coldly. "I had just about managed to put that cruel memory behind me. And now it lives again."

But, as usual, his carefully honed sarcasm was completely lost on her. "Listen, I've got to go before it gets too hot," Lilly said.

"Can we at least get together after your run?" he asked, pleading.

"Sure," she said, but her voice sounded as if her thoughts were already far away. "I'll see you around, Oliver."

And Lilly hung up.

Oliver tossed his phone on the coffee table and slumped on the couch. How had this happened? Why had his two best friends deserted him?

After a few minutes spent staring glumly at

the ceiling, he slowly got up from the couch. He vaguely knew that he needed to find someone who was a kindred spirit, someone who would be supportive and understanding, someone who could help him through this incredibly confusing time.

Without quite realizing what he was doing, Oliver soon found himself heading for Rico's. When he arrived, he was glad to see there weren't any other customers at the moment. He slid onto a stool at the counter and ordered a strawberry-banana drink from Jackson, who was working the smoothie machine. Once he had taken a few calming sips, he began to pour out his troubles.

"I don't know what I expected this summer to be like," Oliver sighed. "I guess I thought I'd be hanging out all the time with Miley and Lilly, the way we used to, you know? We've always been so tight. And remember how we talked about all the fun we were going to have this summer? We had a plan! It was a good plan! And it involved the three of us being together!"

"Mmm-hmm. I remember." Jackson nodded and started cutting up some strawberries. He'd heard many tales of woe over a strawberry-banana smoothie or a frosty soda, and he knew enough not to offer advice to his customers until they asked for it.

"And then *Talen* came along," Oliver continued, sneering a bit as he said the surfer's name. "And poof! Miley barely has time to answer a text message, let alone go to a movie or hang out on the beach."

"Yep, you're in a tough spot." Jackson began polishing a glass that didn't need it. An idea was beginning to form in his mind, a small but potentially quite useful idea. He nodded encouragingly to keep Oliver talking as he mulled over his latest brainstorm.

"And then all of sudden Lilly decided she should become a pro surfer!" Oliver pushed his dark hair out of his eyes, the better to stare broodingly into his now-empty glass. "So I'm sure I'll never see *her* this summer, either."

"There are plenty of other fish in the sea," Jackson said absently. It was something his father always said when he was upset about yet another girl breaking up with him.

Oliver stared at him, confused. "I *know* there are lots of fish in the sea," he said. "And they're all going to see a lot more of Lilly than I am. That's the point I'm trying to make here, Jackson. I've been abandoned by my best friends!" He held out his empty glass. "Hit me again."

"Sure thing." Jackson plopped banana slices, strawberries, and some yogurt into the smoothie maker and hit the switch. As the machine whirled the ingredients into a creamy swirl, Jackson's mind was working just as fast. By the time the smoothie was done and he had poured it into Oliver's glass, he had a full-blown plan. Like all of his schemes, it was absolutely foolproof and borderline brilliant.

"It's too bad this surfing competition is leaving you out in the cold," Jackson said, his voice oozing with sympathy. "But you should try looking on the bright side."

"There is no bright side," Oliver muttered, staring down into his smoothie. He lifted the glass and took a big swallow. "There is only darkness and loneliness and despair." He slammed back the last of his smoothie and held out his glass to Jackson again.

Jackson shook his head. "I think you've had enough."

Oliver glared at him.

"It's for your own good, buddy." Jackson started wiping down the counter.

Oliver slumped on his stool and cast a bitter look at Jackson. "You know, maybe there is a bright side," he said, feeling mean. "At least I don't have to waste my summer working at a smoothie bar."

Jackson couldn't have written a better opening if he'd tried. He bit his lip to keep from grinning. "Are you kidding?" he asked, his eyes wide with astonishment. "I'm the luckiest guy in Malibu!"

Oliver's eyebrows shot up in surprise. "How do you figure that?"

"Look around you!" Jackson swept his arm out in an expansive gesture. "I've got a great gig here! I wouldn't trade places with anyone! Not for any amount of money!"

"That's not what you were saying the other day at breakfast," Oliver reminded him. "The other day at breakfast you said your summer was ruined because you had to slave over a smoothie machine—"

"Uh, yeah, right." Jackson thought fast. "I'll let you in on a little secret, Oliver. I said all that to fake out my dad. If he knew how much I loved this job, he'd probably worry. He'd think that I might give up on college, that I might forget about any other career, that I'd end up working at Rico's for the next thirty years."

"Really?"

Jackson was relieved to see that Oliver was buying this story. Now he just needed to put out some bait. "Oh, yeah," he assured Oliver. "Number one, I get to drink all the smoothies I want."

"With any kind of fruit?" Oliver asked, impressed in spite of himself.

"Yep," Jackson said solemnly. "Even mango."

"*Mango,*" Oliver whispered. He had to admit, all-you-can-drink mango smoothies were a definite perk. Then he had a dark thought. "But what about Rico?"

Rico was the son of the surf shack's owner. He was an obnoxious kid who liked lording his power over his dad's employees. Jackson had had his share of run-ins with Rico, and he had never emerged the winner.

But Jackson just smiled. "Off to summer camp," he said.

Oliver nodded. "Sweet."

"And the surf shack is in a primo location,"

Jackson went on, setting the trap. "Right on the beach! My friends are always coming over to hang out, share a few jokes. In fact, I'm pretty much laughing all day long."

In Oliver's lonely state, the idea of being surrounded by friends, talking, joking, having a good time—well, that sounded just about perfect.

Jackson was watching him closely. When he saw the hope flicker in Oliver's eyes, he decided to spring the trap. "And here's the main reason this is the best job on the planet," he said, nodding toward the ocean. "Take a look at that."

Obediently, Oliver turned and took a look.

What he saw made him forget, for the moment, all the suffering that had been visited upon him. Three girls were strolling down the beach carrying surfboards, silhouetted against the sun so that they seemed to be surrounded by a golden halo. As they walked with an easy stride past the snack shop, Oliver saw that they wore T-shirts over their bathing suits that said BREAKPOINT SURF SERIES. Just as he was registering that they were actually *pro surfers*, one of the girls turned and smiled directly at Oliver. She had curly brown hair and laughing brown eyes and the whitest teeth Oliver had ever seen.

"Wow," Oliver said in a hushed voice.

"That's what I'm talking about," Jackson said, satisfied. "California summer, man! Sun, sand, and surfer girls! It's classic."

The girls ran into the ocean laughing, and the spell was broken. Oliver sighed.

Jackson leaned over the counter. "All you have to do is use your moves, Oliver," he whispered, "and this will be a summer you'll remember forever."

"Yeah . . ." For a moment, Oliver was lulled by Jackson's words. For a moment, he was seriously tempted. For a moment, he truly believed what Jackson was saying.

Then he returned to reality.

"But I don't have any moves," he pointed out sadly.

Jackson suppressed a grin. This must be how Uncle Earl feels, he thought, when he goes fishing and one of those big old trout finally bites his hook.

"No, you don't," he agreed. He watched with satisfaction as Oliver's face fell. "At least," Jackson went on smoothly, "not *yet.*"

Oliver eyed him suspiciously. "What does that mean?"

Jackson leaned back against the counter and folded his arms. "I mean," he said, "all you need is someone older and wiser who can show you the ropes, the way Donnie Delray did for me a few years ago."

"Donnie Delray?"

"A legend at my school back in Tennessee, the coolest guy in three counties," Jackson explained. "He taught me everything I know."

He gazed thoughtfully at the horizon as if he were weighing a big decision. After a long pause, he nodded to himself. "Everything I know. And now," he continued, his eyes growing misty, "I think it's time for me to pay it forward. Oliver, I'm going to teach you everything Donnie Delray taught me. In a matter of days, you'll be one of the coolest dudes on the beach."

Oliver hesitated. This was *Jackson*, after all. The guy who had raised practical joking to an art form. The guy who was always working some kind of scheme. The guy who, last time Oliver had checked, was an unlikely candidate for winning a Nobel Prize in Coolness.

On the other hand, this Donnie Delray sounded like he knew what he was doing. And if Oliver could indirectly get a few nuggets of wisdom from him, it might be worth it to go along with Jackson.

"Tell you what," Jackson said. "I'll sweeten the deal for you. I'll even let you take some of my shifts."

Oliver's eyes widened.

"Hanging out with your friends," Jackson said in a hypnotic voice. "Drinking all the mango smoothies you want. Being in the middle of all the action. Imagine it, Oliver! Working at Rico's! The epicenter of summer fun!"

"Yeah," Oliver said slowly.

"In fact—" Jackson pretended to hesitate, then said in a rush, "Oh, what the heck! You can work *all* my shifts!" He clapped Oliver on the back. "Of course, I'll be sacrificing a lot, not being able to hang out here with my friends, so I'll bank the salary. But *you*—" He smiled generously at Oliver. "You can keep all the tips."

From somewhere deep within his brain, Oliver sensed that this logic was flawed, but he couldn't quite put his finger on why. "I don't know," he said slowly. "Maybe I should think this over—"

"Think it over?" Jackson was astounded. "Didn't you notice that girl with the brown hair? She was totally into you, Oliver, I could tell."

"Really?" Oliver's eyes followed the girls, who were now straddling their boards in the blue water, waiting for a wave. Instantly, he made up his mind. "When do we start?"

Chapter Five

Feel the waves and catch a few
Will you catch me? Will I catch you?

Miley, Jackson, and Mr. Stewart had just finished dinner later that night when the doorbell rang. Miley jumped up, her eyes sparkling.

"I'll get it, don't move, it's fine, no problem!" she called out over her shoulder as she flew across the living room.

Jackson and his father exchanged a puzzled look.

"I haven't seen Miley move that fast since the time Uncle Earl asked her to help him clean out the pigpen," Mr. Stewart said.

She skidded to a halt in front of the door and paused to take a deep breath.

Stay calm, Miley, she said to herself, her heart thudding in her ears. Talen is just a guy, you're just doing homework, there's absolutely no reason to be nervous. . . .

Then she caught a glimpse of herself in the hall mirror. Agghh! Living by the sea had one big downside: frizzy hair.

I look like Bozo the clown, she thought in despair. No! Worse! I look like Bozo—on a bad-hair day!

The doorbell rang again.

There was no time to dash to the bathroom for a fast repair job. Frantically, she looked around and spotted a green vase filled with white flowers sitting on the hall table. Perfect!

Miley pulled the flowers out of the vase and dropped them onto the floor.

"Hey!" her father called out. "I just bought those! They were on special at the grocery store!"

Quickly, she reached into the vase, scooped

up some water, and plastered down her hair.

"I try to make the house look nice," Mr. Stewart muttered. "And for what?"

She picked up the flowers, dumped them back in the vase, and opened the door. "Hi!" she said, trying to sound casual.

"Hi, Miley." Talen was wearing blue-and-white surfer shorts, a sparkling white T-shirt, and flip-flops. His hair was slicked back and looked a shade darker than normal. Miley smiled to herself. Maybe she wasn't the only one who had to deal with hair frizz.

He leaned forward to look more closely at her. "Is that a flower in your hair?"

Her right hand darted up to her head and her fingers found the flower. "Oh, yes," she said, trying to laugh. "I was, um, trying out a new look."

He tilted his head to one side. "I like it," he said. "Very retro."

Miley beamed. Talen is so sweet and kind and polite, she thought. It's such a relief to be able to hang out with someone like him, instead of—

"Hey, Talen! I hear you and Miley are going to do *homework* together," a jeering voice said behind her. "That's what she was calling it, anyway. *Homework*."

She whirled around to see Jackson grinning at her. Miley glared at him. "We are!" she said hotly. "We have tons of writing we have to do for Mr. Dickson."

"Oh, yeah, 'cause I know you're *so* into English class," Jackson said, his eyes shining with pure evil. "I guess that's why you have to do makeup work during summer vacation."

Before Miley could follow her natural instinct, which was to somehow make her brother vanish from the planet (permanently, if possible), her father came in from the kitchen and rescued her. "Jackson, weren't you going to take my car out for a spin this evening?" he asked.

Jackson's mouth dropped open. After that

unfortunate (and totally explainable) accident with his dad's car, Mr. Stewart had said he would never let Jackson drive it again. In fact, he said he wouldn't even let Jackson sit in the driver's seat while it was parked in the garage. If Mr. Stewart had his way, he said, he wouldn't even let Jackson *breathe* on his car.

"What? I am? Why?" he asked suspiciously.

"Remember, you were going to listen for that pinging noise in the engine?" His father gave him a meaningful look. "Remember, I told you how it's been driving me crazy and I wanted you to check it out for me? Remember, you agreed you'd drive around until you heard it too, no matter how long it takes?"

Jackson's face brightened as if he'd just won the lottery. Actually, he didn't remember any of this conversation, and he halfway suspected that his father was losing his mind, and he was completely confused about why his dad kept giving him those mysterious looks—but Jackson didn't care.

"You got it, Dad!" he said. "Hand over the keys, I got to hit the road before that ping gets any worse!"

As he grabbed the car keys from his father's hand and headed out the door, Miley shot her father a grateful look. "Dad, this is Talen Wright," she said. "He's in my summer school class."

"Nice to meet you, Talen." Mr. Stewart shook Talen's hand, then paused, his head tilted to one side. "Talen, Talen . . . that's a real unusual name, but I swear I think I heard it somewhere recently. . . ."

"He's competing in the Breakpoint Surf Series," Miley said, cutting her dad off before he could say anything embarrassing about the way she and Lilly had acted when they heard Talen was coming to Malibu. "I thought we could work out on the deck."

"Sure thing, bud, take some sodas out with you," he said easily. "But remember, I want to see some writing going on out there."

"Okay, Dad, thanks!"

And before he could say anything else, she and Talen escaped to the back deck and the warm summer night.

A short time later, Miley and Talen were sitting across from each other at the patio table, their notebooks open in front of them, frosty glasses of soda close at hand. A warm, gentle breeze blew as the sky darkened into a rich, deep blue. Miley glanced shyly at Talen, who was gazing out at the crashing surf. The setting sun had turned his hair gold. Just past his right shoulder, a single star twinkled in the sky.

The night couldn't have been more perfect. So, of course, Miley thought, it was typical that her palms were clammy, her foot was tapping with nerves, and a band of bouncing butterflies had taken up residence in her stomach.

As if he could feel her gaze, Talen turned

and his eyes met hers. She blushed. I hope he doesn't think I was staring at him, she thought. Even though, of course, I *was* kind of staring at him. But it's hard not to stare at him when he's sitting right here beside me looking exactly the way he did in that full-page photo in *Teen Talk* magazine, right down to that dimple in his left cheek and the freckles across the bridge of his nose! It's so interesting that freckles always sound terrible, but then when you see them in real life you realize they're actually quite cute, especially when they look like a light dusting of nutmeg—

"Um, Miley?"

She came to with a start and realized that she was still staring at Talen. "Yes?" she said, inwardly groaning.

But Talen just grinned. "You seemed kind of lost in thought for a minute."

"Oh, right! I was! I was thinking that we should probably get started on our home-work!" she said brightly.

"Sounds good to me," Talen said. "The sooner we start, the sooner we finish, right?"

"Exactly." Miley flipped back to the page where she had written down Mr. Dickson's instructions. "So, let's see . . ." She peered at her notes. "It says tonight we're supposed to 'write, as specifically as possible, about the feelings we have as we engage in our favorite activity—'"

Talen closed his eyes and fell back in his chair with a theatrical groan. "Isn't it bad enough we have to write about this stupid topic every night? Why do we have share our feelings, too?" He said the words "share our feelings" as if he had just bitten into a wedge of lemon.

"I *know*," Miley said with heartfelt agreement. Then she was suddenly struck with a blinding insight: Mr. Dickson's assignment, which she had resented just as bitterly as everyone else in the class, actually had a pretty sweet upside. Namely, she was going to hear about Talen Wright's inner feelings! She was going to learn what mattered most to him! She was going to discover the real Talen Wright, the Talen that even *Teen Talk* didn't have access to!

"But at least we don't have to write on some lame topic like, 'What I did on my summer vacation!'" she added.

"Actually," Talen said, "that would be much easier for me because I'm doing what I do every summer. Surfing!" He frowned slightly. "That's my point about this assignment. I love to surf so I just, you know, surf. I don't spend a lot of time thinking about it. Or thinking about how I feel about it."

"I know," she said sympathetically. "Me neither. I mean, I don't think a lot about singing."

"So that's what you want to do someday?" he asked. He sounded relieved to turn the conversation toward her. "Be a singer?"

"Well, not someday," Miley blurted out. Too late, she bit her lip and corrected herself. "I mean, I just like singing now, you know? Actually, I love it."

He was nodding, interested. "That's great," he said sincerely. "You should keep at it. Who knows, maybe one day you'll even make a CD and become famous!"

"Who knows?" she said, smiling. As she took a sip of soda, she saw her father peering out the kitchen window. "I think we should start doing our journal assignment," she added hurriedly. "Before my dad comes out here and starts lecturing us about the importance of readin', writin', and 'rithmetic."

"Good enough." Talen uncapped his pen with great ceremony and held it poised over a blank sheet of paper. "How. I. Feel. About. Surfing," he recited as he wrote the words on the top of the page. He looked from the page to Miley and back to the page again. He sighed. "This is worse than being held down by a gangbuster wave."

She laughed. "Here, I'll help you." She reached over and put her hand over the page. "Don't look at the blank paper. Just talk to me.

Tell me the first thing you remember about surfing."

He raised one skeptical eyebrow, but he said, "The first thing I remember? Well, that's easy. I was maybe three years old and I was standing on the beach with my mum. We were watching my dad surf. He ran into the water with his mates. They were all laughing and joking and having so much fun. And even though I was just a little kid, I remember thinking, I want to do that someday."

He paused, then added with a grin, "Actually, what I was thinking was, I want to do that *right now*. I want to feel the water and have that much fun. So I ran toward the waves as fast as I could. I could hear my mum yelling at me to stop, but I was a pretty determined little guy. I got far enough to feel the water rush in over my feet. Then my mum grabbed me and started banging on about how a wave could've knocked me down. I completely missed the point, of course, 'cause I remember thinking it would be pretty cool to have a wave hit me."

Talen stopped, an amazed expression on his face. "Wow. I haven't thought about that in, well . . . forever."

"And it was perfect!" Miley said. "Now all you have to do is write it down."

Fifteen minutes later, Miley and Talen put down their pens and made a quick trip to the kitchen for more sodas and snacks. As Miley was foraging in the pantry for a bag of chips, she heard Talen say, "Hey, you don't read this stuff, do you?"

She emerged from the pantry and saw that he had picked up a copy of *Teen Talk* that had been lying on the counter. He was holding it away from him as if it were toxic. "Man, this magazine reeks."

"Oh, yeah, I know," Miley said quickly. "My dad's always bringing celebrity rags home from the grocery store. We keep telling him,

'Dad, get some help!' but he can't resist. It's a sickness, really."

"Maybe he should reach for the gum at the checkout counter instead," Talen said with a faint grin. Then he glanced back at *Teen Talk* and a peevish expression crossed his face. "And this one is the worst! You know what they do? Every month, they make up all kinds of things about me, like my favorite color and my favorite book and stuff like that."

"No!" Miley hoped she sounded suitably outraged.

"Oh, yeah." He nodded. "You can't believe a word they write. And you know what else I hate? They make it look like famous people are always happy and always look great. I mean, take a look at this." He flicked a finger against the cover photo.

For the first time, Miley focused on the magazine enough to see that it was a photo of . . . her!

That is, it was a photo of Hannah Montana,

flashing a brilliant smile at the camera as she arrived at a celebrity awards show.

"You think Hannah Montana actually looks this good when she's just hanging around the house?" he asked.

"Um, well . . ." Miley said, momentarily distracted by the fact that Talen had said she— or, at least, Hannah Montana—looked good. Then she caught sight of her reflection in the kitchen window. Her hair was windblown from sitting on the deck, and not in a cute, my-hair's-just-tousled-for-the-photo-shoot kind of way. More like in a crazy, I-forgot-to-brush-my-hair-for-the-last-two-days kind of way. She quickly ran one hand through her waves and said, "Probably not."

"Check out this headline. 'Down-Home Country Girl Stays True to Her Roots!'" he read out loud. "Huh. Magazines always say that kind of stuff, don't they?"

"But that *is* true!" Miley blurted out.

"How do you know?" he said teasingly.

"Are you friends with her or something?"

"No, but I, um, saw her being interviewed on TV and she seemed really down-to-earth," Miley said. "I don't think she could fake that."

"Well, maybe not," Talen shrugged. "But still, I wouldn't want to hang out with someone who likes me just because of what they read about me in magazines. They wouldn't know the real me at all."

"I can understand that." Miley took the magazine from his hand and tossed it in the trash. "Speaking of which . . . can I read your journal entry?"

"Oh. Well. I guess so." Talen looked oddly uncertain. "If you really want to."

"I do," Miley said, with a reassuring smile. "After all, that's one way for me to get to know the real you, right?"

They returned to the deck, snacks and sodas in hand. Talen handed Miley his notebook willingly enough, but he looked nervous.

"It's really rough," he said. "I just wrote down whatever came into my head. I wasn't trying to make it sound good, it's probably terrible, in fact I *know* it's terrible. Forget it, I shouldn't let you see it. . . ."

He reached over to grab the notebook back, but Miley turned away so he couldn't reach it and kept reading. After a moment, she looked up from the page.

"It's great."

"Really?"

"Really. I love this part"—she flipped back a page—"where you talk about how, when you were little, your dad used to surf with you sitting on his shoulders."

"I'd almost forgotten about that until I started writing, then it just came to me out of nowhere," he said, smiling with relief. He paused. "And . . . thanks. I never would have thought of writing about that day on the beach if it hadn't been for you."

"You're welcome." She handed the note-book back to him.

"So . . . ?" Talen asked in a teasing voice.

Miley looked puzzled. "So what?"

"So are you going to read me what you wrote?" he asked.

"Oh, I don't know. . . ." Flustered, she automatically covered her journal entry with her hand.

"Come on," he said. "Fair's fair."

"Well . . . okay." She cleared her throat and began to read. "'I've loved music since before I was born. My dad tells me that when my mom was pregnant with me, he used to talk to her stomach, hoping that I could hear him. When he was talking about his day or the plans he had, he said I never seemed to react too much. But when he'd sing to me, my mom swore I was moving to the rhythm of the music—and that I kicked a little harder when I heard Elvis! I think that music was always inside me, just waiting to come out.'"

When Miley finished reading, she kept her eyes on the page, afraid to look up and see Talen's reaction. She hadn't told anyone that story before, not even Lilly, and she didn't think she could stand it if Talen thought it was stupid or boring or . . .

"I like it."

She peeked at him from under her eyelashes.

He nodded at her. "You're a good writer. And that's a great story."

"Thanks." Miley felt a surge of relief, quickly followed by a surge of self-doubt. "You're not just saying that?"

"Nope," he said definitely. "And it also has nothing to do with the fact that I am the world's biggest Elvis fan."

She grinned. "I think my dad might want to arm wrestle you for that honor. And you definitely don't want to take him on." She leaned forward and whispered, "He cheats."

"I'll be happy to claim the title of *Australia's* biggest Elvis fan," he said with a cheerful shrug. "As long as you promise to sing 'Hound Dog' for me some day."

"Deal," she said, laughing.

For a few moments, they sat next to each other, their feet propped up on the railing, watching the surf in a friendly silence.

Finally, Talen said, "I'm glad we got together tonight."

Miley didn't dare look at him. Talen Wright was glad they got together! She kept her eyes fixed on the rolling surf and tried to remember how to breathe.

But then he kept talking, this time through a mouthful of chips. "I don't think I would have been able to sit down and write all those pages if I was by myself. It really helped to talk it through with you."

See what happens when you go and jump to conclusions? Miley scolded herself, a bit crestfallen. Of course he was only talking about doing homework together!

"Oh, good," Miley said, sounding as off-hand as possible. "Maybe we could do it again. Get together, that is. Just to do homework, of course. And only if you want to." Finally, she managed to stop talking.

Talen didn't answer right away. But just as the silence had stretched out so far that she was actually hoping her father would come out and tell them they had to call it a night, Talen turned to her, smiling. "Of course I want to," he said. "I mean it, Miley. I had fun. You're so different from the last girl I hung out with."

"Oh, really?" Miley said. *Which girl was that?* She was quite proud of how casual she managed to sound, considering.

He stretched his legs out and stared into the darkness, nodding. "Jessica—you know, in class?—we dated for a while. I don't know if you figured that out."

"It was kind of obvious that you guys had a history," Miley said dryly.

He gave her a smiling glance. "I think that's

a nice way of saying that she acts like she hates my guts."

Miley looked away from him. And then, before she could think about whether she should ask the question looming in her mind, she heard her own voice say, "So, what went on between you two guys, anyway?"

There was another long silence. Miley winced. How could you ask such a personal, private, nosy question? she thought in despair. Now he's going to hate me! Why, why, why couldn't I keep my mouth shut?

But then, to her surprise, he chuckled. "Well, we started dating about a year ago, when she first joined the circuit," he said. "I'm such an idiot. It took me months to figure out that the only reason she went pro was—"

He stopped in midsentence and blushed.

A blushing Talen was even more charming that a regular Talen, Miley thought. Which was saying a lot.

"'The only reason she went pro was . . .'"

Miley prompted as gently as possible.

He shrugged and said, "Well . . . to meet me. 'Cause I'm kind of, I don't know . . ." He wouldn't meet her eyes. "Famous, I guess."

How sweet, Miley thought, to be embarrassed about being a superstar surfer! Most guys would be bragging about that day and night.

"But why does she hate you?" Miley couldn't imagine it. "It was because you broke up with her, right?" She did her best to sound sympathetic, although secretly she was delighted by this idea.

"Well, actually she broke up with me," he admitted.

"Oh." Miley's heart sank. She should have known! Talen probably still had a thing for Jessica! He was heartbroken over the breakup! He couldn't wait to get back together with her! "So, if she broke up with you, why is she mad at you?"

He shrugged in frustration. "Good question. See, I thought we were hanging out 'cause we liked each other. But after a while, she started winning competitions, and then magazines started treating us like some kind of super surfing couple. Jessica loved that. She started trying to get me to buy all kinds of stupid stuff and live like a celebrity's supposed to live, and I didn't want to do it. So she broke up with me, but she's still kind of mad that we're not together, getting all that attention." His voice trailed off. "So, anyway. Lesson learned. That was the first time I realized how people can try to use you if you're a celebrity."

"That's terrible!" Miley said fervently. "Awful! You're better off without her!"

He laughed. "Yeah, I think so, too. At least I don't have to listen to her banging away all the time about how I should spend my money on better clothes or a nicer watch instead of—" He stopped abruptly.

"Instead of what?" Miley had to ask.

"Oh, just this project I have," he said off

handedly. "I set up a fund to help some people who are working to save the Great Barrier Reef. It's off the coast of Australia and it's just the most awesome place—" He stopped again, as if afraid he had said too much, and shrugged. "I know I sound like a real goody two-shoes. . . ."

But Miley had already melted. "Not at all," she sighed. "In fact, I think you sound . . . noble!"

He laughed. "Yeah, that's me, Sir Talen."

"No, really," she insisted.

"I just don't think people need so much stuff, y'know? I mean, look at that." He gestured toward the ocean.

Miley looked. Waves crashed on the shore, foam gleaming white in the moonlight. Stars twinkled in the velvety black sky overhead. A soft breeze cooled the warm summer night. She sighed.

"Life's perfect as is, don't you think?" he added. "No accessories needed."

She turned to look at him, mesmerized by his earnest blue eyes, his deep, philosophical nature, and his unbelievably selfless spirit. "Yeah," she sighed. "Perfect."

Chapter Six

No time to think, no time to fear
Now it's time to take the dare

"Good morning, Dad!" Miley said the next morning as she danced into the kitchen. "Isn't it a beautiful, fantastic, wonderful, perfect day?"

"Sure is," he agreed. He gave her a long look. "You sound mighty chipper."

She shrugged blithely. "Well, the sun is shining, the birds are singing—"

"And you're getting ready to go to yet another day of prison . . . oops, I'm sorry, summer school," Jackson reminded her as he stepped into the kitchen from the deck. He shook his head in mock sorrow. "Hunched over a desk for hours while your friends live the California dream. I feel for you, Miley, I really do."

"Thanks, but, actually, summer school is great," she said cheerfully.

"Great? What happened to 'but, Dad, it's going to ruin my entire summer'?" Mr. Stewart asked.

"Oh, please, I was so much younger when I said that!" Miley protested. "I've matured since then!"

He raised one eyebrow in disbelief. "That was just a few days ago."

"As I said," she responded happily, "*so* much younger."

Before her father could pursue this any further, there was a knock on the door and Oliver bounded in. He was wearing lime-green surfer shorts that were a little too big, a screaming yellow shirt, and bright orange flip-flops.

"Morning, everybody!" he said.

Jackson crossed his arms and gave Oliver a long, considering look. "Hmm. I see we have some work to do. It looks like a box of crayons exploded in your closet."

"Oh." Oliver looked down, as if seeing himself for the first time. "I borrowed these things from my dad. He wore them when he surfed, back in the day—"

"That explains so much," Jackson said. "Don't worry, little dude. I'll take you to the surf shop this afternoon and get you fixed up."

"What's going on here?" Miley asked. For the first time, she noticed her older brother's clothes. He was wearing a white rash guard to protect his skin from the surfboard's rough surface. He had on green-and-white baggies that looked brand-new. And his look was topped off with a puka-shell necklace and flip-flops. "What's with the costume?"

"It is not a costume," Jackson said. "Oliver and I are going surfing this afternoon."

"You?" Miley said. "Are going into the ocean?"

"That is the best place to catch a wave, last

time I checked," Jackson said loftily.

"Catch a wave?" Miley couldn't help it; she dissolved into giggles. "You're kidding, right?"

Jackson glared at her. Oliver glanced back and forth between Miley and Jackson, a look of worry on his face. "Why would he be kidding?" he asked. "Jackson said that if I helped him out at Rico's—"

Mr. Stewart rolled his eyes. "Please don't tell me he's talked you into doing some of his work, Oliver. Please don't tell me that."

"Yes, but it's okay. I *want* to!" Oliver said earnestly. "Because in return, Jackson's going to teach me all about riding the waves . . . Miley, what's so funny?"

But Miley was laughing too hard to answer.

Jackson appealed to their father. "Dad! Tell her to stop!"

But Mr. Stewart was trying to hide a grin of his own. "That's like telling someone to stop hiccuping, son," he said. "Can't be done."

"I don't get what's so funny." Jackson

crossed his arms, mortally offended.

"You won't go in the water past your knees, you scream every time a wave hits you, and you're afraid of sharks and jellyfish," Miley said, catching her breath.

"Of course," her father said, trying to be fair, "everyone's scared of sharks and jellyfish."

Oliver glanced nervously from Miley to Jackson. "Um, Jackson," he said hesitantly, "you have surfed before, right?"

"Dude, that is totally the wrong question to ask," Jackson said with great assurance. "I mean, just take a look at me." He held his arms wide and paraded around the kitchen as if he were a model on a runway. "Do I *look* like I can surf?"

"You look like you could beat Talen Wright," Oliver admitted. "But—"

"Thank you!" Jackson threw his hands into the air with a gesture that said he had proven his point. "And that concludes your first lesson in coolness, Oliver. Appearances are more important than reality. If we *look* like surfers, people will think we *are* surfers. Got it?"

Reassured, Oliver grinned. "Got it!"

As they headed out the door, Miley and her dad looked at each other and shook their heads sadly.

"Oliver will just have to learn the hard way," Mr. Stewart said. "If you want to be cool, you should never ask Jackson for advice."

"Ya think?" Miley said, rolling her eyes. She abandoned the topic of Jackson without ceremony and moved on to a subject slightly more dear to her heart. "Just so you know, Daddy, Talen and I are going to hang out after school for a while, then we're going to do homework together again. Oh, and I asked him to come to dinner, so I hope that's all right! See ya!"

She turned to run out the door, her footsteps light, her heart singing.

"Hold on a minute," her father said. "Aren't you forgetting something?"

Miley froze in midstep. "I don't think so,"

she said. "Heading for school, check. Hanging out with Talen, check. Doing homework together, check . . ."

Her dad shook his head. "Meeting with the costume designer to get ready for your concert," he reminded her. "Check and double check."

Her eyes widened. "Oh, no, that's not today!"

"'Fraid so, bud. You need to go to the designer's studio right after school," he said.

For one brief moment, Miley thought about protesting. She thought about whining. She thought about complaining.

But then she remembered: in a little over a week, she was going to put on a concert. She'd be onstage, singing her heart out, hearing the cheers and applause from hundreds of fans. She knew that she didn't have it in her to argue. After all, she loved performing. Getting fitted for new costumes was part of her job.

Not to mention the fact that dressing up in glittery new clothes was also extremely fun.

Her eyes gleamed as she began to imagine what the costume designer would have come up with for this show. Then her mind wandered to Talen—cute, kind Talen—and her heart wavered a bit.

"You've got to make tough decisions when you're in show business, Miley," her dad reminded her.

Miley sighed. She let herself visualize, just for a second, how great it would have been to spend all afternoon at the beach with Talen.

Then she let that go and focused instead on how great it would feel when she was onstage performing—in a brand-new costume, no less. "You're right," she said. "After all, I can hang out with Talen tomorrow."

But when Miley got to class, she immediately felt a twinge of regret. The first thing she saw was Jessica sitting on Talen's desk, swinging her tanned legs and leaning over him so that her long hair fell just so.

Jessica noticed Miley slipping into her seat and gave her a smile that reeked of insincerity. Then, with a toss of her head, she turned back to Talen and said, rather more loudly than necessary, "You know, I thought movie stars were supposed to live in Malibu, but I haven't seen one famous person since we got here. I haven't even seen a *semi*famous person."

"Well, we *are* here to surf," Talen pointed out. "Not to meet movie stars."

"I'm tired of surfing all the time," Jessica complained. "Listen, Talen! Tonight we're all going to head over to LA to see if we can find something fun to do."

"Oh, yeah? You've cleared that with Mr. Robinson, I suppose?" Talen asked skeptically.

She sniffed. "Yes, and *of course* he insisted on going with us as a chaperone. He says it's to protect us, but *I* think he just wants in on the fun." She tossed her head again so that her hair swung through the air in a shining, multicolored arc. "Even Mr. Robinson, who invented boredom, thinks Malibu is boring."

"I think Malibu is fine." Talen leaned back a few inches to keep Jessica's hair from getting in his eyes. "Even if you don't, no need to keep whining about it."

"But, Talen, you really ought to come with us," Stefan, the redheaded surfer, chimed in. "What's the point of being on a world tour if you don't see some of the sights?"

"I *am* seeing the sights," Talen said mildly. "I'd rather see the ones right here in Malibu, that's all."

Jessica's eyes flickered in Miley's direction. "Oh, right, I forgot," she said. "You always like to check out the *local* talent, don't you?"

Talen flushed angrily at that and opened his mouth to say something. It was probably fortunate, Miley thought, that Mr. Dickson interrupted by clearing his throat and saying, "Okay, class, let's get started. How did everyone do with your journal writing last night?"

☆   ☆   ☆

Miley was glad when the class finally ended and she could walk out the door with Talen. The class discussion had been torturous, to say the least. No one had wanted to read a journal entry out loud, so Mr. Dickson had resorted to lecturing them at length about the need to be emotionally open and honest in their writing. This was a topic that he cared about a great deal—or at least that's what Miley assumed, since he managed to talk about it for almost the whole class without taking a breath.

When he finally stopped, blinked, and looked around the room, he saw that Dan was fast asleep with his head on his desk, Jessica was twisting her hair into a dozen small braids, Jackie was staring vacantly out the window, and most of the other students were doodling in their notebooks.

He was so annoyed that he told everybody to write an extra three pages that night. "Open and honest pages, people!" he added. "And there *will* be reading aloud tomorrow, so be warned!" He ignored their groans.

The only good thing was that he released them half an hour early, into the bright afternoon sunshine.

"So what do you want to do before we hit the books?" Talen asked. "Maybe catch a wave or two?"

Miley was so shocked by this suggestion that she completely forgot she had another appointment. "But I don't surf!" she blurted out.

He grinned. "Even better. I can teach you."

Her mouth fell open. Talen Wright? Was offering to teach *her*? To surf?

"Um, well, I don't know," she said weakly, even as her mind flashed through every bathing suit she currently owned and quickly calculated that it was not remotely possible to wear any of them in front of Talen, which meant that an emergency trip to the mall had to happen right now, this afternoon, as soon as she . . .

Oh. Right. The costume-designer meeting.

"Come on," he was saying. "It'll be fun. And you'll be perfectly safe, don't worry. After all, I'll be watching out for you."

"It sounds great, but I meant to tell you earlier. I have, um, something else I have to do this afternoon," Miley said.

"Oh." He nodded, but his expression was distant. "Sure."

"No, really!" she said quickly. "I'd love to learn to surf, because I really love the ocean, and I've always loved watching the surfers from our house, and there's nothing I'd love more than for you to teach me. . . ."

Miley replayed what she had just said in her head, and winced. There she was, using that "love" word again. She *really* had to watch that.

The good news was that Talen's expression was no longer remote; in fact, he looked relieved.

"But I do have this appointment that I can't cancel," she said more calmly. "So can I have a rain check? Maybe for tomorrow after class? But you can still come for dinner tonight if you want."

"Sure," Talen said. "Sounds good. And no worries. We'll get you out on the water soon enough."

"Thanks." Relieved, Miley gave him a quick wave and headed off, pulling her cell phone out of her purse as she went. She was so intent on calling Lilly that she didn't see Jessica lingering nearby, frowning at Miley as she walked away.

Chapter Seven

I'm standing tall, I'm flying free
Now I've found a whole new me

"I'm so excited to be working with you, Hannah," said Josslyn Jones, the costume designer hired by Mr. Stewart, as she flew across the room. She was a tiny woman with shoulder-length black hair, who seemed to quiver with barely suppressed energy.

"Your manager and I agreed that you need a very special costume for the very special final number in this very special concert."

"You talked to my da- -my manager about my costume?" Miley asked with a sudden sinking feeling.

For this meeting, she was, of course, wearing

her long blond Hannah wig, full makeup, and a glittery top and denim skirt from the secret Hannah side of her closet. It was amazing what a difference clothes could make in how a person felt, she thought. She always felt so much more "on" when she was dressed as Hannah Montana: more confident, more in control, more in charge.

But the news that her manager—who also happened to be her fashion-challenged father— was involved in choosing her costume caused those warm feelings to vanish.

"Oh, yes," Josslyn said, staring intensely into Miley's face. "We've had many long talks. He has such interesting ideas . . . well, quite frankly, they're not just interesting, they're inspirational. I've already mocked up several designs. And I've been so *invigorated* by this project that I find my brain is simply flooded with ideas, from the moment I wake up until the moment I drop, in complete creative exhaustion, to sleep." An expansive gesture with her right hand came close to clipping Miley on the ear. "Your costume will speak of the sun sparkling on the ocean and the moon in the dark night sky! It will speak of barbecues on the beach and fruit drinks on the sand! It will speak of youthful high spirits and sweet summer romance!"

"That's one talkative costume," Lilly muttered to Miley.

Miley gave her a warning look. "This is my friend Lola Luftnagle," she said to Josslyn. "She always comes to my costume fittings."

Lilly had met Miley at the studio dressed in her own disguise as a member of Hannah Montana's entourage. A quick change into a blue-and-white-striped top and white capri pants, topped by one of Lola's many colorful wigs had transformed Lilly, surfer girl, into Lola, daughter of a fabulously rich oil baron and Hannah Montana's BFF.

Josslyn gave Lilly one quick glance, said, "Fabulous hair; lime is absolutely your color," and turned back to Miley. "On to business! Are you ready to be *stunned*?"

"Always," Lilly answered for her friend. "We simply *adore* being stunned."

"Then wait here while I get the first costume from my workroom!" Josslyn hurried away.

Lilly turned to Miley. "I can't wait to see how your outfit speaks of fruit drinks on the sand."

Miley giggled but quickly regained her composure. "Shh, she'll hear you," she whispered. "Where in the world do you think Dad found her? Take a look at this place!"

Together, she and Lilly walked slowly around the studio. The table in the middle of the room was covered with fabric swatches in headache-inducing shades of pink, yellow, green, and blue; the dress form by the window displayed a dress with a long, ragged hem trimmed with seashells; and many of the sketches pinned on the walls seemed designed for a punk-rock version of *The Sound of Music*.

"Well, she's certainly . . . original," Lilly said, trying to sound positive.

But Miley was feeling more nervous by the minute. "She's been getting creative direction from Dad! You know what that means. Remember the dress he bought me for the winter dance last year?"

Lilly nodded somberly. "It looked like it was made from a poinsettia tablecloth," she said. "And the corsage that lit up? That will be talked about at every school reunion for the next fifty years."

"You don't need to remind me." Miley closed her eyes in remembered pain.

Then she heard Josslyn say, "Ta-da!"

Miley opened her eyes to see the designer standing in the doorway of her workroom holding a pineapple, an expectant look on her face. "What do you think? Really, I want to know! Don't hold back! I love constructive criticism! What is your true, honest, heartfelt opinion of this?"

Miley stared at her. Her mind was blank. She *had* no opinions about pineapples. She never even knew she was *supposed* to have opinions about pineapples. "Well, I—"

Before she could go any further, Josslyn held up one hand to interrupt her. "But what am I saying?" the costume designer asked the room. "How can you know what you think if you don't see the full effect?"

She turned to snatch a drawing from the wall. Miley breathed a sigh of relief. "The full effect" sounded promising. Maybe the pineapple motif was going to be worked into a fabric design or serve as the inspiration for some funky earrings—

Her eyes focused on the sketch that Josslyn was now dangling in front of her face. Then they widened in shock.

"What . . . is . . . that?" Miley asked weakly.

"Your headdress for the big number at the end of the show!" Josslyn said, beaming. "It's fantastic, don't you think?"

The pineapple served as the base for a towering hat made of fruit. Cherries and grapes clustered around the bottom, a banana curved like a feather plumed on the back, and kumquats pinned into a small orange pyramid formed the top.

"Well, it looks tasty," Miley began, trying to be diplomatic.

"And healthy," Lilly added, smirking. "Filled with vitamin C." Miley shot her a glance, and Lilly put on a straight face again. "Also very, very summery," she added, trying to be helpful.

Josslyn gave a sigh of relief. "Oh, thank goodness! I was so worried you wouldn't like it, after I worked around the clock for three days to create it! You just don't know how relieved I am to find out that you truly share my vision!"

Great, Miley thought. Other costume designers have visions of glamour and sparkle. My costume designer has visions of fruit bowls.

"I'm just a little bit worried about how it will hold up during my routine," she said carefully. "I'm not sure it's really, er, *practical*."

As criticism went, Miley thought that was rather well-phrased. It was diplomatic, it was honest, it was mild.

But despite Josslyn's claims that she longed to know what Miley really thought, this mild comment seemed to strike her to the heart. The designer's eyes filled with tears. "I knew you would hate it!" she wailed. "I knew it!"

"No, no, I don't hate it!" Miley hurried on. "I just don't want to see something so creative and, um, unusual be destroyed by accident!"

Lilly nodded vigorously and pointed to the dozens of other sketches. "It looks like you came up with tons of designs," she said. "Isn't there anything else that would work?"

Josslyn gave a sad little sniff. "Nothing will work as well as my pineapple headdress," she said mournfully. "It is"—a tear trickled down her cheek—"*unique.*"

"Oh, I'm sure someone as talented as you will be able to design something else just as good," Miley said hurriedly. "Or even better! My da—that is, my manager told me that he hired you because you were one of the best costume designers in the country!"

Josslyn sniffed again, but she looked a little mollified. "Well, that's true," she admitted. "Possibly one of the best in the world."

"Exactly!" Miley was relieved. She felt she had pulled Josslyn back from the brink of despair *and* managed to avoid wearing a pineapple. So far, so good. Now, if only there were a fantastic, showstopping costume among all these sketches. . . .

"Well, I have nothing quite like this, of course." Josslyn took one last, mournful look at the headdress sketch, then firmly put it aside. "But I do have several ideas that are almost as fun! Just wait here!"

She again disappeared into the depths of her workroom. Miley grinned at Lilly. "That was a narrow escape," she said.

"No kidding." Lilly picked up the pineapple and perched it on top of her head, then walked slowly over to a full-length mirror so that it wouldn't fall off. She tilted her head to one side, then the other, making the pineapple wobble alarmingly.

"Be careful!" Miley whispered. "If that thing falls, we'll be cleaning pineapple juice off the floor for days."

"Okay, chill," Lilly said, putting one hand up to steady the fruit. "I just wanted to see how I would look onstage as Hannah Montana." She struck a pose, smiled maniacally into the mirror, and drawled, "Hey, y'all! Thanks for coming!"

"Ha-ha, very funny." Miley marched over and took the pineapple off her friend's head, setting it down on the table with finality. "So, what's been going on? I feel like I haven't seen you in forever."

"I know!" Lilly said. "Practicing for the

competition has been crazy. I'm wiped by the end of the day. You know, last night I fell asleep at the dinner table? I only woke up when my face landed in my mashed potatoes."

"Ooh, I hate it when that happens," Miley said. "Especially when you get gravy up your nose."

"Or butter in your eyebrows," Lilly said, laughing. "But Jessica said I need to practice as much as possible. Even in the novice class I'm going to be competing with primo surfers."

"Jessica?" Miley frowned slightly.

"Yeah, you know her," Lilly said casually. She moved to the middle of the room, balanced on her left foot, and slowly brought her right foot up in front of her. "She said she's in your class. She's a good friend of Talen's."

Good friend? Is that what she tells people? Miley almost said this out loud, but she was distracted by the sight of Lilly grabbing her right foot in her left hand and stretching her other hand toward the ceiling.

"What are you doing?" Miley asked.

Lilly was gazing into the distance, her eyes narrowed with concentration as she tried to hold her pose. "Yoga," she said through barely opened lips. "Jessica said it would help my balance on the surfboard. She's been giving me some tips."

"What kind of tips?" Miley was so surprised, she said this a little more sharply than she had intended. Startled, Lilly promptly fell over.

"Ouch," she said, glaring up at Miley from where she had landed on the floor.

"Sorry. But we are talking about the same Jessica, right? The one with blue and green and pink hair? And all the earrings? And the attitude? Are you really taking her advice about . . . about *anything*?"

Lilly stood up and brushed herself off. "Well, when it comes to surfing, yeah. She's been on the pro circuit for a couple of years, so she knows a lot about competing and how to impress the judges." She started over with her yoga pose. "If you want, you could come with us for burgers tonight. I think you'd like her if you got to know her a little bit better," she added casually.

Yeah, and pigs might fly to Uncle Earl's farm and build condos on his back forty, Miley thought.

But she just said, "Thanks, but I've got other plans."

Lilly was staring straight ahead, focusing fiercely on keeping her balance, but she still managed to raise one eyebrow. "I bet. Do those plans have the initials TW, by any chance?"

Miley couldn't help grinning. "Yes, as a matter of fact! Talen's coming for dinner tonight. And guess what? He's going to teach me to surf."

"Oh, really?" Lilly said in a teasing voice. "I thought you didn't want to learn how to surf."

Instantly, Miley remembered all the times she had adamantly refused Lilly's offers to teach her. She shot her friend a guilty glance and said lamely, "Well, no, I didn't, not before, but now . . . I guess I do."

"Sure." Lilly managed to sound worldly wise and knowing with just that one little word.

"Well, he *is* a world-class surfer," Miley said defensively. "And you know how klutzy I am. I figured I need someone who's a professional to teach me, otherwise I'd probably end up hurting myself!"

"That's true," Lilly said. She was now grinning from ear to ear. "Remember that time you tried to shoot a free throw and the ball bounced off the rim and hit you right in the face? That was classic. Or when you turned a cartwheel and crashed into the bleachers? Oh, and remember when—"

"Yes, thanks for the highlight reel, Lilly," Miley said, pretending to be annoyed.

"You've got to let me know when you're having your first lesson," Lilly went on cheerfully. "Really, I'll pay admission to watch."

They were both still giggling when Josslyn swept back into the room.

Miley stopped laughing abruptly. Josslyn's arms were filled with what looked like . . . could it be . . . *straw*?

But maybe she was mistaken. Maybe the costume was cutting edge, maybe it was fashion forward, maybe it wasn't really that bad. . . .

She glanced over to check out Lilly's reaction and saw that her friend was trying, not very successfully, to hide a wide grin.

It *was* that bad.

"Now here is another creation I came up with in a burst of inspiration the other night!" Josslyn cried. She held the costume out to Miley. "Please! Try it on! I can't wait to see how you look."

"Neither can I," Lilly said, a wicked gleam in her eye.

Reluctantly, Miley took the costume into the dressing room. A few moments later, she emerged and stared into the mirror in disbelief. She was wearing a bikini top that looked like coconut halves (cunningly made from foam and bark material) and a full hula skirt that hung almost to her ankles. She could see Lilly's reflection behind her as her friend tried desperately not to laugh.

"Voilà! Hannah Montana goes Hawaiian!" Josslyn cried in triumph.

"It's a new look for you," Lilly murmured, a glint of laughter in her eye. "I like it."

"Yeah," Miley said forlornly. "Just call me Hula Hannah."

From Miley Stewart's Journal

My first memories all involve music. I remember sitting on the back porch on warm Tennessee evenings, watching the fireflies flicker in and out of the darkness. It was before we moved to Malibu, and things were quieter, simpler. My dad would sit in his old rocking chair, the one my granddad made that had all the paint worn off from sitting in the sun for years. He would be picking out a tune on his guitar if he was working on a song. But most of the time he'd just relax and sing all the old-time country songs he'd heard his father and mother and aunts and uncles and grandparents sing when he was growing up.

I can remember my mom sitting on the porch swing, smiling at my dad, tapping her toes to the rhythm of the music. That was just about the only time I ever saw her sit down and do absolutely nothing. During the day she was always busy, making the beds, mowing the lawn, cooking meals, feeding the horses, making sure the house hummed along in a neat and orderly way.

But at night, when the supper dishes were done, she'd come out onto the porch and listen to my dad's guitar as the moon rose in the sky, not doing anything, her hands still in her lap, just smiling at us and sometimes humming along.

Chapter Eight

Just believe, life will go your way
Anything can happen on a summer day

"Let's go over this again." Jackson stood on
the beach in front of Oliver, his arms folded,
surveying his pupil with a challenging stare.
"What's our primary directive?"

Oliver gulped and tried to look confident.
For the past week, when he wasn't working at
Rico's, he had been enrolled in what Jackson
insisted on calling "Jackson's School of Cool."
This meant being lectured by Jackson, doing
homework assigned by Jackson, and taking
pop quizzes given by Jackson.

Oliver would never have believed it, but it
turned out that learning to be cool was almost

as tedious as studying the Industrial Revolution. Possibly even more so. At least the Industrial Revolution had involved steam engines. And sometimes they exploded.

Jackson's School of Cool, on the other hand, involved memorizing forty-two "Cool Rules," not to mention various directives, principles, and corollaries to said rules.

Some of them—like Rule #1 (don't smile too much), Rule #2 (don't talk too much) and Rule #3 (don't wave your hands around too much)—were easy enough to remember.

But Oliver kept forgetting Rule #23 (don't bob your head while listening to music). He kept flubbing Rule #31 (don't trip over your own feet). And, after spending hours studying Jackson's Cool Rules, he found the last rule (relax!) absolutely impossible to follow.

But today, finally, despite Oliver's shaky memorization skills, Jackson had decreed that it was time for him to stop studying theory and put what he had learned into practice. . . .

"Oliver!" Jackson snapped. "Pay attention. I asked you to state our primary directive!"

. . . after one final exam, of course.

Oliver sighed, but answered. "Always act cool."

"Correct." Jackson gave a quick little nod and fired another question. "And what are the three major principles of talking to a girl?"

"Make eye contact," Oliver recited dutifully. "Act like you're interested in what she's saying. And, um . . ."

He furrowed his brow as he tried to remember the last principle. He could practically see the page of his notebook where he had written it down, but it was hard to remember with Jackson giving him that gimlet-eyed stare. Oliver felt beads of sweat break out on his forehead, and he began breathing heavily through his mouth.

"Here's a hint," Jackson finally said. "Your hair looks great."

"Really?" Oliver's worried face broke out in

a smile. "Thanks, Jackson! I tried a new gel this morning—"

"No, no, no!" Jackson yelled. "I didn't mean *your* hair looks great! I meant *her* hair looks great!"

Oliver glanced around wildly. The beach wasn't crowded yet; no one stood anywhere near them. "Who are you talking about? Whose hair? Where?"

"That's the third principle, Oliver," Jackson said through gritted teeth. "Pay her compliments! Like, your hair looks great, that's a wicked T-shirt, you're a good dancer—"

"You've got great math skills!" Oliver said, finally catching up and eager to join in. "I like the way you smell! Awesome shoelaces!"

There was a brief silence.

"Okay, sure," Jackson said, shaking his head. "Whatever works, man."

Then his eyes shifted past Oliver and brightened with interest. He murmured, "Check it out. Gidgets at three o'clock."

Instantly, Oliver's head swiveled to the right.

"Don't—" Jackson began in a strangled voice.

But it was too late. Oliver had made eye contact.

"Sorry," Oliver said. "Really, really sorry."

"Never mind." Jackson gave a martyred sigh. "Watch and learn." As he started toward the girls, he called back over his shoulder, "Feel free to take notes."

He sauntered up to them and said, ever so casual, "Hey."

All three girls smiled at Jackson. "Hey," they said in unison.

Oliver shook his head in admiration. Jackson's technique was working!

"I'm Jackson."

It was hard for Oliver to believe that this was an opening line that had required hours of rehearsal. Still, it seemed to work. The tall girl with short blond hair, who looked a little older than the others, introduced herself as Pamela. The girl with black braids said she was Annie, and the short girl with brown hair—the one whose smile was permanently seared into Oliver's heart—introduced herself as Daphne.

"We've been hanging out with the same bunch of surfers for so long, we can finish each other's sentences," Annie offered. "It's nice to meet someone new."

"Oh, really?" Jackson immediately broke Rule #1 by breaking into a huge grin. "You surf?"

Pamela rolled her eyes ever so slightly at that, but her friends seemed friendlier. "Yeah," Annie said, with a nod at her surfboard. "Actually, we're on the tour."

"Cool." Jackson nodded. Oliver could tell he was trying not to seem overly impressed, but he forgot to stop nodding. Just when it looked like he was turning into a life-size bobblehead doll, he managed to recover enough to say, "Well, let me know if you need info on the surf around here. I'm a local, you know."

Pamela grinned slightly at this. "Really? Well, in that case . . . we were just about to go in. Why don't you and your friend join us?"

"Oh, I would, but, um . . ." Jackson stumbled to a halt, his mind clearly blank.

Oliver rescued him. "We just ate. Need to wait an hour before swimming. Cramps, you know." He grabbed his side and winced to illustrate his point.

Jackson's face lit up with relief. "That's right. Can't be too careful."

Pamela's lips were pressed together as if she were trying not to smile, but she nodded. "Too bad. Well, some other time, then. Do you guys usually hang out in this spot?"

As Jackson continued to talk to Pamela and Annie, Daphne turned to Oliver. "Hi," she said. "I think I remember seeing you the other day at that little snack place. What's it called?"

She remembered him! Oliver wondered if he was going to faint.

"Rico's," he managed to blurt out.

"That's it!" She beamed and waited expectantly for him to elaborate.

He smiled back, dazed. It seemed that he had mysteriously lost the power of speech.

After a long moment of silence, she asked, "So . . . what's *your* name?"

Good question. He tried desperately to think of the answer.

Finally, out of the dim recesses of memory, it came to him.

"Oh! My name's Oliver."

From the corner of his eye, he saw that Jackson was still talking. A lot. In fact, he was babbling on as if he'd just eaten a whole bag of Halloween candy in one sitting and then washed it down with a few energy drinks. Not only that, but he had started waving his hands around to emphasize what he was saying.

However, the other two girls didn't seem to mind the fact that he was breaking Rules #2 and #3 with abandon. In fact, Annie was laughing at whatever he was saying, which Oliver took to be a very good sign. Even Pamela was looking less superior and more amused.

"Well, I've got to go practice," Daphne said. "Maybe I'll see you around? On the beach?"

"Sure, great," he managed to say.

She picked up her surfboard and ran toward the ocean. At the last moment, she turned to wave. "See you later, Oliver!" Then she plunged into the water and was gone.

"What did I tell you?" Jackson loped up to him, grinning with satisfaction. "When your diploma is from Jackson's School of Cool, you're going to rule the beach—guaranteed!"

Chapter Nine

In your heart you feel the sea
Ride the waves and you feel free

Miley could hardly wait for English class to be over. She had been so preoccupied with thoughts of her first surfing lesson since dinner with Talen the night before that, at one point, Mr. Dickson had to call on her three times to get her attention. He had frowned with annoyance; Miley had blushed with embarrassment; Jessica had smirked with satisfaction. Fortunately, Talen had glanced across the aisle just then and given her a sympathetic smile.

Miley lifted her chin and answered Mr. Dickson's question, thinking, so what if Jessica laughs at me? Talen and I are going to hang out all afternoon. And I'm going to learn to surf!

Instantly, she was lost in a happy daydream about how cool she would look as she rode a wave in her brand-new fuschia bathing suit, a daydream that lasted until class ended for the day.

As soon as Mr. Dickson dismissed them, she jumped up, eager to get to the beach. But the teacher chose that moment to say, "Talen, I wonder if I could have a word with you?"

Talen sighed. "Sure, no problem," he answered. The students had quickly learned that when Mr. Dickson wanted to have a word, it usually meant writing extra journal pages that night.

Now it was Miley's turn to give him a sympathetic look. "I can meet you later," she said. "How about down by the jetty?" That was a spot strategically chosen to be as far from Rico's—and Jackson's mocking gaze—as Miley could get.

"Excellent," he said, before reluctantly

heading up the aisle to Mr. Dickson's desk.

As Miley left the classroom, she heard the teacher say, "I'd like to discuss your last few journal entries, Talen. They seem to be, shall we say, a little on the brief side—"

Then the door swung shut, cutting off his voice.

In a way, Miley thought, she was glad that Mr. Dickson had held Talen behind. That would give her time to get to the beach and put on her wet suit, which she had borrowed from Lilly, without him seeing.

She had planned to try on the wet suit the night before, but then Talen had called to discuss their homework, and they had ended up talking for an hour (five minutes about the latest assignment and fifty-five minutes about everything else under the sun). They would have kept talking all night if Talen's cell phone hadn't lost its charge and if Miley's dad hadn't pounded on the door and yelled for her to get downstairs.

After that, Miley had had to write in her journal, then Lilly had called to talk about her surfing practice that day, then her dad wanted her to listen to a new song he was writing for her concert, and before she knew it, it was time for bed.

Now, as she headed toward the beach, she found herself humming a new tune that she had started composing that morning. In fact, she had awakened with the tune running through her head, so perhaps she had discovered it in her dreams. It was fun, with a bright swing and bounce that sounded like summer to Miley. She hummed a little more, trying to hear the words that seemed tantalizingly just out of reach.

"The first thing I noticed were your beautiful eyes," she sang softly under her breath. Hmm, not quite right. "First I saw your laughing eyes," she tried again.

This task was so absorbing that, before she knew it, she was at the beach, where the first person she saw was Oliver.

"Yo, brah," Oliver called out. He grinned at her, incredibly pleased with himself.

"What?" Miley asked, totally confused. Was that actually *Oliver*?

"That's how surfers say hello," Oliver explained. "Jackson taught me that. Cool, huh?"

"Oh, yeah. Very." Miley just managed not to roll her eyes. After all, Oliver was her friend, and he was terrific in many ways, but even she knew that he shouldn't try to sound like a hip surfer. There were so many, many ways that plan could go wrong. "But I think I liked it better when you started every conversation in Spanish."

"Man, that's so old school," he said with disdain.

Miley looked him over. He was wearing a black rash guard, red baggies, and cool new sunglasses, and he was holding a surfboard. It was obviously a very old surfboard—Jackson had probably scrounged it up for him from the surfers' version of a Goodwill store—but the battered condition actually made Oliver appear to be someone with a lot of surfing experience. He looked, she had to admit, a million times better than he had the other morning . . . but she knew the truth. No matter how he dressed, he was still Oliver.

"Yo, brah, howzit?" a voice yelled from behind her.

Miley whirled around to see Jackson bounding up, carrying his own surfboard.

Miley couldn't believe it. After all her planning to make sure she and Talen had some alone time, she had to run into these two! "Jackson! What are *you* doing here?"

Jackson smiled smugly. "Checkin' out the surf situation," he said.

Oliver nodded in solidarity. "Waitin' for some tasty waves."

Miley glanced past them at the ocean, which was filled with surfers. Some were paddling out, some were waiting for waves, some had caught a wave and were speeding toward shore, but there was one thing they all had in common. . . .

"Then maybe you should get in the water?" she said pointedly. "Just a suggestion."

Oliver and Jackson exchanged uneasy glances.

"Well, actually, I told my mom I'd get home early and help her fix dinner," Oliver said. "Tonight's lasagna, and those noodles are tricky."

"Yeah, I think it's time we ducked," Jackson agreed quickly. "But tomorrow we'll rip some waves for real."

"Yeah, be sure to let me know when that happens," Miley said dryly. "I'll want to bring my camera."

"You got it," Oliver said, failing to notice Miley's sarcasm. "Well, I'm peacin', brah. See ya tomorrow."

As he and Jackson headed down the beach, Miley pulled Lilly's wet suit out of her backpack. She held it up in front of her. It looked pretty tight-fitting, but she'd shimmied into her fair share of spandex as Hannah Montana. How hard could this be?

Fifteen minutes later, out of breath and red-faced, Miley was about to cry.

First, she had tried to put her feet through the legs of the wet suit while standing up. Of course, she had promptly fallen over and gotten covered with sand. Even though she tried to brush it all off, enough of the grains had stuck to her skin to be irritating. After two more attempts, and two more falls, she finally realized that she should sit down on her towel and pull the wet suit on from that position. After several minutes, she managed to pull it up to her knees, but then she had run into another obstacle.

Lilly, it seemed, was a bit smaller than she was.

Miley had never noticed this before—in fact, if asked, she would have said that she and her best friend were close to the same size—but the evidence was clear. As she tugged futilely to get the wet suit past her hips, she started sweating, which only made matters worse. And then, when she had finally managed to work the suit up as high as her waist, Jessica strolled up.

Great, Miley thought grimly. Just what I need, a visit from the Wicked Witch of the Waves.

"Need some help?" Jessica asked, not even trying to conceal her smile.

"Me?" Miley did her best imitation of a carefree laugh. "Thanks, but I'm fine." She gave another quick tug to the wet suit, which stubbornly refused to budge.

"Everything—" Another tug.

"is under—" And another.

"control."

Aagghh. Somehow the rubber had gotten bunched up around her waist.

Jessica tilted her head. "You sure about that?"

Miley could feel the sweat running down her forehead, but she forced a smile. "Absolutely. No worries here!" Another tug. Still nothing.

Jessica shrugged. "Okay." She started to leave, then turned back. "You *do* know that the zipper goes in the back, right?"

As she walked away, Miley stared down at the zipper and muttered, "Sweet niblets."

"Okay, time to learn step number one." Talen turned his head toward Miley. He was lying down on his surfboard, the blue sky forming a perfect backdrop for his blond hair, his blue eyes, his white teeth. . . .

"Miley?"

"Um, yes, what?" she stammered. "I am! I totally am!"

"You are what?" he asked, puzzled.

"Ready to learn how to surf! So let's get to it!" She smiled brightly, hoping without any conviction that he hadn't noticed the way she had been staring dreamily at him.

She had long since given up on the wet suit. Instead, she was wearing her bathing suit and a rash guard she had borrowed from Talen, and she was lying on her stomach on top of her own surfboard, also provided by Talen.

"Okay, then," he said. " Ready and—jump!"

In one fluid movement he leaped to his feet and stood perfectly balanced on his board. At the same moment, Miley jumped up, over-balanced, and sprawled . . . onto the hot sand.

"Oh . . . grits and gravy!" she sputtered in frustration.

Talen had started her lesson by having her practice the most basic move—jumping from a prone position to a standing position on the surfboard—while still on the beach. And it was a good thing, too, she thought. If she'd actually been in the water, she'd have been dunked more than a dozen times.

As it was, she was merely covered with an ever-increasing layer of sand.

"Why is this so hard?" she complained as she tried, without success, to brush herself off. "And how do you make it look so easy?"

"Well, I *have* been surfing for most of my life," Talen said. "And you've been surfing for, um, let's see . . . an hour?"

"Good point," she said, her irritation vanishing in the face of his good humor. "But I don't know if you can really call it surfing, since I haven't even gone into the ocean yet."

"Don't worry, you're doing great," he said encouragingly. "Come on, one more try."

Miley sighed, but again stretched out on her surfboard.

Talen did the same. "So pretend you're in the water," he said. "You're paddling out—" He started paddling with his arms, making the sand spurt into the air.

Miley giggled, but she imitated him. "Okay, I'm paddling. . . ."

"And you see a wave coming," he went on. He pointed ahead of them. "Look, there it is!"

Miley looked, pretended to spot the wave, too. "I see it!"

"Okay, get ready and—jump!" he yelled.

She didn't give herself a chance to think. Miley jumped . . .

. . . and she was standing on the surfboard!

"Yee-ha!" she said. "I did it!"

"That's awesome, Miley," Talen said. "See, it's not that hard once you get the hang of it."

Before Miley could enjoy her moment of triumph, another voice from behind her said, "Yeah, you're doing great—if you plan to surf on the sand, that is."

Miley looked over to see Jessica standing a few feet away, smirking at her. "It's nice of you to spend so much time with a newbie, Talen," Jessica went on. "But shouldn't you be practicing? After all, the first heats are in a few days."

"Chill out, Jessica," Talen said. "I know when the competition starts."

"Hmm." She readjusted her ponytail. "If you

say so. I'd just hate to see you lose because you were too"—her gaze rested on Miley for a moment—"distracted."

"I'm not distracted," Talen said firmly. "And I don't plan to lose."

Jessica shrugged. "We'll see about that," she said, glancing down the beach. She interrupted herself to wave to someone. "Oh, hey!" she called out in a lively voice. "You were really rippin' out there, girl! Way to go!"

The switch from snarky to friendly was so sudden that Miley had to turn to see who Jessica was talking to. The sun was in her eyes, so it wasn't until the other surfer had jogged up to them that she realized Jessica's friend was . . . Lilly!

"Thanks, Jessica!" Lilly was breathless from jogging up the beach, but she was beaming. "That was so much fun!"

A few other surfers had drifted over. Miley recognized them: they were all on the surfing tour with Talen, they were all guys, and they were all totally cute. And, right now, they were all openly admiring Lilly.

"That was righteous," one said.

"Wicked," another agreed.

"Totally radical," a third added.

"Yes," Jessica said, a little more coolly. "Lilly is doing quite well. For a novice."

Lilly was glowing. "Thanks to *you*," she said to Jessica. "It's all those pointers you've been giving me. I think they've really helped."

Jessica thawed slightly. "Well, I like helping people who are new to the sport," she said, flicking a quick glance at Talen to see whether he was impressed by this selflessness.

"Careful with that halo," he said, deadpan. "You wouldn't want to lose it in the surf."

"Very funny," she said, scowling. She turned back to Lilly and added, in a more businesslike voice, "And as soon as you correct your stance, you'll have a good chance to win your first heat. Or at least come in a respectable second."

Lilly's smile dimmed. "What's wrong with my stance?"

"Well, I wasn't going to say anything yet, because I didn't want to hurt your confidence," Jessica said smoothly. "But since you asked, it's just a little bit too wide."

"It is?" Lilly looked worried. "I thought it was fine. . . ."

"Oh, it is," Jessica said smoothly, "for an amateur. But if you want to *win*—"

"I do, I do!" Lilly said quickly.

"Then let's get in one more set before it gets dark," Jessica said, picking up her surfboard, "and I'll show you how to fix it."

The three surfer boys were already racing each other across the beach. When they reached the water, one of them turned around and waved.

"Come on, Lilly!" he called out.

"Gotta go," Lilly said hastily to Miley. "See you later."

She ran into the ocean, dived under the

breakwater, and paddled out to join them. Miley watched as Jessica called out something to Lilly, and Lilly laughed and yelled something back. A soft breeze lifted a lock of brown hair across Miley's face, and she reached up to push it away, feeling strangely invisible.

Don't be ridiculous, she scolded herself. Remember, you're the one who gets all the attention when you're Hannah Montana, and Lilly always supports you and never stops smiling. . . .

The hair tickled her nose. She reached up to bat it away—and found that she was swiping at a long piece of beach grass.

She looked up to see Talen smiling at her in an understanding way, even as he tickled her nose with the grass again. "Hey, I just had a great idea. How about joining me on dawn patrol tomorrow?" he asked.

Miley gulped. "As in dawn? As in really, really early in the morning?"

He grinned. "Yeah, but there's no better

time to go surfing, believe me. It's really fun."

Fun? For a split second, Miley thought about getting up at sunrise, jumping into freezing cold water and trying to surf, which was something she had never done in her life. There were so many reasons to say no, she couldn't even begin to list them all. . . .

Then she looked into Talen's bright blue eyes. He nodded encouragingly. "Trust me," he said. "You'll love it."

So Miley, feeling reckless and brave, nodded. "Okay," she said. "Tomorrow at dawn."

From Miley Stewart's Journal

When I was in elementary school, I started singing along to the radio and to the records we had around the house. Sometimes I'd make my friends sit on the couch and be my audience. They'd applaud and cheer and I knew right then that nothing felt better than performing, nothing.

For a while, music was just something I liked to play at. Then one of my grade-school English teachers made us write poetry for an assignment. Most people in the class hated it. But when I wrote my first poem, I realized I was also writing a song. I discovered I could tell people how I felt about things and make them understand it through my words. That felt like such power to me.

I started trying to write music by picking out tunes on the piano or on my guitar. Pretty soon I would wake up in the morning with a song already humming in my head.

Or I'd have an idea for a lyric while I was at school, and all I could think about was how long it would be before I could go home and write it down.

Or I'd hear somebody say something in a catchy way, and I'd think, that would make a great hook for a song.

It made me notice the world in a way I never had, because I started to look at everything—the birds in a tree, my best friend's new red dress, the mud puddle in the driveway—and try to figure out how I would write about it in a song so that everybody would see what I saw and understand how I felt about it.

♪♪ Chapter Ten

Falling under, lost in the tide
But there you are, right by my side

Dawn was not nearly as bad as Miley had feared it would be.

True, when her alarm clock went off, she thought it was the middle of the night. She woke with a start and looked around her dark bedroom, flailing in vain to hit the snooze button.

However, the night before she had deliberately moved her alarm clock to the other side of the room for this very reason. Muttering under her breath, she threw her legs over the side of her bed and staggered across to where the clock was chirping cheerily, as if mocking her for having to get up at—she squinted incredulously at the dial—*five o'clock in the morning?*

But even as she groaned and hit the snooze button a little harder than necessary, her brain was whirring into gear.

Talen, she reminded herself hazily. You're getting up early so you can meet Talen.

That thought gave her enough of a jolt to get her into the bathroom, where she turned the shower on full blast.

"Agghh!" The shower's spray was icy cold. Miley lunged for the hot water faucet and twisted it as far as it would go.

From Jackson's room next door, she heard a sleepy shout. "Keep it down, wouldya? Some of us are trying to get our beauty sleep!"

"Hate to tell you this, Jackson," she yelled back, "but no amount of sleep is going to make you beautiful."

The only reply was a muttered grumble that sounded like a grumpy bear rolling over after being awakened during hibernation.

Miley grinned to herself and leaned her head back, enjoying the feeling of hot water. Finally, *finally* she seemed to be waking up. Stepping out of the shower, she craned her neck to peer out the bathroom window. Dimly, she could see that the black sky was lightening to indigo.

"Surf's up," she told herself, excitement beginning to stir. "Let's go."

"Come on, Miley," Talen yelled. "Duck under the wave and kick!"

Miley bit her lip as she stared out at the churning breakwater in front of her. Then she thought, Just do it, already! What's the worst thing that can happen?

Before she could consider the answer to that question—which was either drowning or looking like a fool in front of Talen—she took a deep breath, grabbed either side of her surfboard, and pushed below the water that was hurtling toward her.

A few very long seconds later, she popped

up on the other side of the breakwater, taking deep gulps of air and blinking saltwater out of her eyes. She flung her hair back and looked around the gently rolling sea for Talen.

"That was great!" he yelled, waving at her from where he sat on top of his board a few yards away. "You look like a pro already. Ready to rock these waves?"

Miley gulped, but smiled brightly. "Sure!" she called back. "Whenever you are."

He looked out to sea, his eyes narrowing as he watched the incoming swells. "I'm just waiting for the right wave," he yelled to her, his gaze still fixed out to sea. "It might be a few minutes."

"That's fine with me!" she yelled back. "No worries."

Miley relaxed a little as they floated side by side, getting used to the rocking of the ocean underneath her, the waves gently lifting her up and down. The sun was still rising, and the sky above her was deep blue with just a thin band of gold on the horizon. In a few hours, she knew, the sunlight would be blazing down on a hot California summer day. But now . . . now the world was lit with a soft glow that blurred the edges of everything.

And in a few hours the air would be filled with the sound of laughter, music being played full-blast on the beach, and children screaming with delight. But right now she could hear even the smallest sounds: the water lapping at her surfboard, the distant cry of a seagull, the flag on the shore rippling in the breeze. She shivered, partly from the cool air, but mostly from sheer delight. The world looked brand new, and she and Talen were the only people awake to see it.

"Here we go, Miley!" Talen called out.

Her eyes widened as she saw the large wave that was coming toward them. It seemed to tower over her, blocking out the sky.

"Go on, paddle out to meet it!" he yelled.

Miley flopped down on her board and

began paddling with all her strength. After all, she hadn't dragged herself out of bed and struggled into that stupid wet suit just to give up at the first wave, had she?

No, she answered herself with grim determination, she had not.

But the wave, she couldn't help but notice, was now looking bigger and more menacing.

She could hear Talen yelling, "Paddle harder! Give it everything you've got!"

Panting, she paddled as hard as she could. Then Talen yelled, "Now jump up on your board, Miley! Do it now!"

The wave was cresting over her. Miley let out a squeak of dismay. She distinctly remembered learning how to do this move yesterday. But faced with a wall of seawater rushing at her, she instantly realized that it had been far, far easier to do it on dry land.

"Jump, Miley! Jump!"

She held her breath, leaped up, and twisted around so that she would be facing forward on her surfboard. Then the wave came crashing down over her head. She was underwater, flailing around with the desperate knowledge that this was it, she was about to drown—

And then her head popped above the surface. She took in a deep, ragged breath and looked around at the world she thought lost to her forever. The first thing she saw was Talen paddling toward her, a huge smile on his face.

"That was awesome, dude!"

"What?" She shook her head to get the water out of her ears. She couldn't have heard him correctly. He couldn't have said that what just happened—getting knocked off her board and nearly dying—was *awesome*! "I wiped out!"

He held out a hand to help her back on her board. "Hey, everybody wipes out their first time. But you jumped up and actually got on the board for, like, a split second." He saw her doubtful look and nodded vigorously. "Honestly. That was excellent."

Miley blinked. The saltwater was stinging

her eyes. "Well, it didn't *feel* excellent," she said, but she was smiling. "It felt scary."

He reached over to pat her shoulder. "You're a champ. You'll get used to it."

Her smile disappeared. "How will I get used to it?" she asked suspiciously.

He looked surprised. "When you try again."

She opened her mouth to protest, but he was already looking back at the ocean. "The surf's great this morning. We should get another wave for you pretty soon. You have to learn how to choose the right one, something that's big enough to pick you up and take you in, but not so big you lose control."

But I don't want to choose a wave! a little voice inside Miley's head cried out plaintively. *I don't want to get used to wiping out! And I don't want to—*

"Start paddling, Miley!" he yelled. "That's a great wave; it's got your name written all over it!"

She watched the wave coming toward her.

It seemed to blot out the sky.

You're a champ, she told herself firmly. That's what Talen said. And if you can sing to a sold-out arena, you can certainly go out to meet that wave.

She took another deep breath and started paddling.

Thirty minutes later, she had tried to catch a wave approximately fifteen times. She had fallen off her surfboard at least five times (and been knocked off by a wave ten times). She was tired, frustrated and for some reason she couldn't quite figure out, very, very happy.

"Get ready," Talen called out. "The next one's yours."

Miley nodded, her stomach jumping. Getting onstage in front of thousands of screaming fans was a walk in the park compared to this, she thought.

A wave rose up on the horizon.

Don't think, Miley. Go.

She started paddling toward the wave as it rose up in front of her, a towering wall of water.

Distantly, she heard Talen yell for her to jump up on her board.

She didn't hesitate. She jumped; she was standing—she was actually doing it. . . .

And then, once again, she felt herself falling off her board. This time, however, she was plunged deep underwater.

Instantly she was in another world, a world with no sound, no air, no control.

She felt her leg jerk as the leash that tied her ankle to her surfboard broke, and then the force of the water pushed her down even farther.

Miley's eyes popped open and she started swimming, desperate for oxygen.

But her lungs were burning, and she no longer knew which way was up. She was suddenly filled with terror at the thought that she might be pulling herself deeper into the cold ocean water.

Then someone grabbed one flailing hand,

and she was being pulled up, up, up. . . .

Miley burst out into the sunlight and took a deep, grateful breath.

"Okay?" Talen asked, breathless.

She nodded, still gasping for air.

He grabbed his board, sat on it, then reached out to take her hand. "Yeah, you're okay," he said. His tone was warm and reassuring.

She managed a weak smile and pushed strands of wet hair out of her face. "Thanks," she finally said, after her heart finally stopped racing.

"For what?" Talen asked.

"Oh, you know." Miley waved one hand in the air, trying to keep her tone light. "For saving my life and everything."

"It's pretty scary, the first time you're held down by a wave," he said. "You want to take a break?"

Grabbing her own board, Miley pulled herself up and pushed a strand of wet hair out of her eyes. "Maybe for just a minute."

"Okay, let's just sit on our boards and"—he swept a hand toward the horizon—"take in the view."

For a few minutes they sat on their boards again and watched the waves. The sun had fully risen, and the sky was now a cloudless turquoise. Three birds swooped past and out to sea, as if in a race to see which one could reach the other side of the ocean first. Miley's body felt tired but light, as if she could float into the sky.

She sighed. "I wish we didn't have to go to summer school today."

"I know," Talen said. "Sometimes I wish I were a dolphin or something, so I could live out here in the ocean all the time." He gave her a quick, embarrassed glance.

"You look like you belong out here," she said, taking in his sun-bleached hair wet with saltwater, and the easy way he sat on his surfboard, as if it were a part of him.

"That's *exactly* how I feel when I'm in the

ocean," he replied eagerly. "Not just surfing. Swimming, snorkeling, whatever; it's like the water is my true home." He gave her another sidelong look. "I don't know if that makes any sense. . . ."

"Oh, yeah," Miley said, thinking of how she felt onstage in front of an audience. "It does. It's like . . . that's where you were born to be."

"Too right!" he said. "Y'know, that's what it means to be a soul surfer. Someone who's not into surfing for fame or money. Someone who just wants to ride the waves under the open sky."

Miley reached over and splashed him playfully. "Hey, that's what you should write in your journal," she said.

"What?"

"What you just said! It was perfect." After a moment she added thoughtfully, "Actually, it would make a great song."

"I'll leave that to you," he said. "When I

sing, even the seagulls get scared. Come on, you want to catch one more wave before we have to go in?"

Miley tried to repress a sigh. Why not end the morning with one last wipeout?

"Sure," she said, trying to sound like she was up for anything.

Talen was already scanning the waves. "There you go," he said, pointing. "That's the best wave of the day! Make it a good one!"

Miley took a deep breath.

She paddled.

She waited for the wave to crest.

She jumped up. . . .

And she was surfing! Balanced on her board, feeling the power of the wave beneath her feet, hearing Talen cheering her on . . .

Then she fell off.

But for a few brief, shining moments, she had known what it felt like to fly free on a wave. And she couldn't wait to do it again.

From Miley Stewart's Journal

I remember the day my dad first overheard me singing one of my songs. I was sitting on the back porch. I didn't think anybody was around, and I really put my heart and soul into the singing. When I finished, I heard someone clapping. I turned around and saw my dad smiling at me.

"That's nice," he said.

"It is?" I asked.

"You bet," he said, nodding. "You sound like you're turning into a pretty good songwriter."

"I am?" I remember how amazed I was to hear my dad say that. After all, he was a songwriter! He had worked in the music business! He had even written some hits!

"Sure enough." He gave me a little wink. "Just keep at it. That's the secret when you have talent. Keep working on it all the time, even when you want to run."

When he went into the kitchen to get a glass of buttermilk, I sat on the porch. I remember how I felt, like I was lit up from inside, like fireflies lighting up the night.

Chapter Eleven

Play it cool, that's your style
What's behind the secret smile?

"Nice work, Talen," Mr. Dickson said as he handed Talen's journal back to him. "I think you've had a breakthrough in your writing. Your description of the morning light over the ocean was quite evocative."

Miley caught his eye, and they exchanged a private smile. Neither one of them saw that Jessica had noticed the smile and picked up on the hint of a shared secret. As her eyes narrowed in displeasure, Mr. Dickson went on, "And I had never heard the phrase 'soul surfer' before. It's a fascinating concept. In fact, I think it might be worth some class discussion time—"

"Excuse me." Jessica's hand shot up.

Mr. Dickson suppressed a groan. In just over a week, Jessica had proven to be one of those students who always had something to say. And while he encouraged class discussion, Jessica's contributions never added much since they always seemed to focus on the same topic: herself.

Still, at least she was willing to talk. He squared his shoulders and nodded at her. "Yes, Jessica?"

"I was just wondering how creating a line of Talen Wright swim trunks fits into the 'soul surfer' lifestyle?" she asked innocently.

Miley's eyes widened in surprise as every head in the class swiveled in Talen's direction. Talen hadn't mentioned anything to her about commercial endorsements!

Of course, she thought, trying to be fair, she hadn't mentioned anything to him about *her* double life as Hannah Montana. But somehow it felt strange to be on the other side, to be the person in the dark instead of the person who was keeping a secret.

"Dude, did your manager finally close that deal?" Stefan grinned. "Sweet."

"Oh, yeah, didn't you hear?" Jessica was clearly enjoying herself. "He's got a photo shoot this afternoon. I heard the company wants to make a whole series of Talen Wright posters, too."

Stefan leaned across the aisle to give Talen a high five. "Way to go, man! That should earn you some serious scratch!"

Talen returned the high five with somewhat less enthusiasm. "I don't even care about the money," he began, looking uneasily across the aisle at Miley. "That's not really the point—"

"Then what is?" Jessica's voice was edged with venom. "Maybe you just like knowing that every girl in the country will have your picture on her bedroom wall?"

Miley winced. Last month she had taped a

magazine photo of Talen—a great shot of him standing on the beach—on the wall next to her closet.

"Of course not." Talen glared at Jessica. "This is just some promotional deal my manager dreamed up."

"Who cares who dreamed it up?" Stefan asked cheerfully. "I'd give anything for a merchandising gig like that."

Jessica raised her eyebrows. "What about your endorsement deal with the surfboard company, Talen? Was that your manager's idea, too?"

Miley frowned. She thought Talen just wanted to ride the waves under the open sky! How did surfboard endorsements and Talen Wright swim trunks and poster photo shoots fit into that dream?

"They're really good surfboards!" Talen said defensively. "In fact, they're great, the best I've ever used—"

"Of course they are," Jessica said, her eyes

gleaming with delight at getting a reaction from him. "You'd never recommend a surfboard if it didn't have 'soul,' right?"

Mr. Dickson cleared his throat loudly. "Remember the class rules, everybody," he said. "We want open and honest discussion in here, not personal attacks."

"I wasn't *attacking* anyone!" Jessica protested. "I was merely asking Talen to define 'soul surfer' a bit more precisely. For those of us"—she smirked at him—"who aren't quite *clear* on the concept."

"Yes, well." Mr. Dickson glanced at his watch. "Looks like we're out of time for today. Let's pick this up tomorrow, all right?"

Talen hurried to catch up with Miley as everyone poured into the hallway after class. "I hope you didn't fall for Jessica's tricks in there," he said when he reached her side.

Miley kept walking.

"Miley?" He sounded worried. "You didn't

believe all that stuff Jessica was saying, did you?"

Miley stopped and turned to face him. "I don't know what to believe," she admitted. "After all, I don't really know you that well."

"Hey, come on!" He tried to laugh. "Of course you know me! I'm Talen, remember? Talen Wright?"

"Is that the Talen Wright who gets up to see the sun rise?" she asked, her voice sharper than she had intended. "Or the Talen Wright who has to run off to a photo shoot for his new line of money-making posters? Just curious because it's a little unclear."

Before he could respond, a mocking voice interrupted. "Hey, Talen. Are you practicing looking soulful for the camera?"

Jessica skipped down a few steps to stand next to them, one hand on her hip, her head cocked to one side.

He scowled darkly at her.

She shook her head in mock sorrow. "You

may want to work on that expression just a *little* bit more," she said. "I'm not sure it will sell too many posters."

"I gotta go," he said abruptly. "I'll call you tonight, Miley."

Before Miley could respond, he was gone.

For a moment, Miley stood still in the late afternoon sunlight, her mind whirling with confusion. Did she want him to call? What would she say if he did? And why was she so upset? It wasn't like he had *completely* lied. Still . . .

"Don't beat yourself up, Miley," Jessica said. "It's not your fault you fell for Talen's humble act."

"I don't think it's an act," Miley said loyally, despite the shiver of doubt she felt. "Okay, so he's famous and he makes a lot of money. He still cares about all the right things, like his friends and the environment—"

"Oh, so he told you how he's planning to save the Great Barrier Reef?" Jessica sniffed.

"Yes, a little bit," Miley said. Even in the midst of her bewilderment, the memory made her smile.

"Of *course* he did," Jessica murmured. "That works on all the girls."

"Including you, I guess," Miley said, stung. "Since you used to date him."

Jessica shrugged. "I'll admit, I fell for it, too. But that's why I'm giving you the 411 here. Because after a while, I learned the truth about Talen."

"Which is what?" Miley snapped.

"That for someone who's always talking about 'keeping it real,'" Jessica said coolly, "he's very good at faking it." She spun on her heel and marched away.

As Miley's eyes followed Jessica's retreating back, her watch beeped. She had thirty minutes to get to the tech rehearsal for her concert. It was time to transform herself into Hannah Montana and forget, for a while at least, about the troubles of Miley Stewart.

Chapter Twelve

Soul surfer, you go your own way
Or is that just something it sounds good to say?

Miley, dressed as Hannah Montana, was rehearsing on a temporary stage that had been built on the Malibu beach. As her band played behind her, she finished her song with a few dance moves that ended in a triumphant pose, with one hand raised over her head and the other pointing at the sold-out crowd.

Or, at least, where the sold-out crowd would be on the night of the actual show. For now she was singing her heart out to rows of empty seats, which was always a slightly weird experience. Still, she'd done this enough times that she could imagine the fans jumping up and down, cheering and applauding wildly.

She smiled at the thought and bowed to the folding chairs. "Thanks for coming!" she yelled. "I love y'all!"

"And they're going to love you," a voice said from the side of the stage. She turned to see her father. As always when he accompanied her as Hannah Montana, he was also in disguise. In his case, that meant a fake mustache, a dark wig, a cowboy hat, and a new identity as Hannah's personal manager.

He turned to the band. "Take a break, guys. I think we're done here." He looked back at Miley. "I was a little worried about scaling down your show for a smaller stage, but it looks great."

"Thanks," Miley said. She flipped her long blond Hannah hair back from her face and fanned herself with her hand. "I just had to learn a few new dance steps, that's all. And I really love my new outfit."

She glanced complacently at her yellow-

and-white sarong skirt, sandals, and white top. It had taken days of argument to convince her father that his fashion sense was nonexistent, and days of tactful persuasion to get Josslyn to create some new choices, but it had been worth it. The resulting outfit was summery, flirty, and fun.

"I still think that hula skirt woulda been real cute," her father drawled mournfully.

"I know you do, but I'm not wearing beach grass onstage," Miley said firmly. "Or any other kind of vegetation, including any and all types of fruit," she added, just to be clear. That pineapple headdress still haunted her dreams.

As the members of the band walked off-stage, Lilly came bounding up.

"Nice hair," Mr. Stewart said to her.

"Thanks." Lilly tossed her head proudly. Today she was wearing a pink wig as part of her Lola Luftnagle disguise. "That was a great rehearsal," she said to Miley. "Practically as good as a real concert."

"Cool," Miley said. "It felt good. I just hope it goes that well tomorrow night—"

Before she could finish, a chipper voice called out, "Hannah Montana, you do not have a thing to worry about! You are *fabulous!*" A short, blond woman wearing extremely high heels came skittering across the stage toward them, smiling maniacally.

"Oh, hi, Cyndi," Miley said, trying to muster up some enthusiasm. "Nice to see you again."

Cyndi Sellars was the endlessly upbeat publicist for the Breakpoint Surf Series, who had— according to Cyndi herself—been working night and day setting up press interviews and photo shoots with the surfers. Now she had Hannah Montana in her sights. Miley knew that talking to reporters and posing for the paparazzi was part of her job as Hannah Montana. But she had discovered, two minutes after meeting Cyndi, that the woman's energy was extremely daunting and exhausting.

"You are the most talented singer I have heard in all my *fifteen years* in the business! Your voice is simply *awesome*! I'm sure you have an absolutely wonderful, wonderful, *wonderful* career ahead of you!"

"Thank you." Miley smiled politely, then changed the subject. "Didn't you say there was going to be a writer from *Entertainment Insider* here today?"

"Yes, indeed, she's waiting for you back-stage," Cyndi trilled. "Come along and I'll introduce you."

She glanced at Lilly and added vaguely, "Oh, and you too, dear, whoever you are."

Behind her back, Lilly rolled her eyes comically at Miley.

As they followed Cyndi off the stage, Miley mentally prepared herself for the interview. The questions reporters asked were almost always the same, and so were the answers:

Are you excited about the concert? Yes, of course!

What do you have planned next? I'm going to take a break, then my manager and I will talk about when to go on tour again.

Enough about work, let's talk romance! Are you dating anyone special? No, I'm too busy to date right now.

Instantly, pictures flashed through her mind. Hanging out with Talen at Rico's. Doing homework together. Sitting on their surfboards, talking as they watched the sun rise. . . .

Stop thinking about Talen, she scolded herself. You're Hannah Montana right now, and you have a job to do.

As she, Lilly, and Cyndi rounded the corner, Miley saw the *Entertainment Insider* reporter, holding a mini-tape recorder and standing next to a photographer. Then her eyes flicked past them and she stopped dead.

Talen was standing next to the reporter! And he was looking her way! In fact, he was smiling right at her!

Miley gasped. For one awful second she forgot to breathe as a million thoughts ran through her head.

Was this the moment her secret was finally going to be discovered?

And what would happen if Talen realized that superstar Hannah Montana was really just ordinary Miley Stewart? Or worse, that Miley wasn't the average girl she claimed to be? Would he hate her for lying to him? Would he call her a hypocrite for being upset with him? And worse, would he think she had wanted to use his fame to boost her fame, just like Jessica had done?

Then she noticed that Talen's smile looked a little more hesitant than usual. He was shuffling his feet, as if he were nervous. And there wasn't even a tiny spark of recognition in his eyes.

She sighed with relief and started breathing again. He didn't know who she was! Her secret was safe.

Cyndi grabbed her elbow and hustled her over to the others. "I have a big surprise for you!" she said. "Talen Wright, meet Hannah Montana! And Hannah Montana"—she whipped out a copy of *Entertainment Insider* and held it up triumphantly—"meet Talen Wright!"

The magazine had a photo of Talen on the cover. The cover line read, "Talen Wright, Australia's Supercool Soul Surfer."

"Hi," Miley said, smiling uncomfortably. "Nice cover."

"Hi," he said. "Thanks."

There was a long silence as Talen stared at her. He didn't look at all like the Talen she knew. His eyes were glazed, his mouth was hanging open slightly, and he seemed to have entered a light trance state.

"I guess these kids are a little shy," Cyndi said to the reporter with a tinkling laugh. She gave Miley a meaningful look and made little pushing movements with her hands, urging them to move closer together.

Miley took a teeny step toward Talen. He looked as if he might faint.

Cyndi clucked with exasperation and leaned over to whisper in Miley's ear. "Honey, this is a great photo op that I've arranged for you. *Don't blow it.* Just look happy and I'll get you and Talen on every magazine cover in the country, guaranteed."

Gritting her teeth with embarrassment, Miley inched a little nearer to Talen.

"Okay, let's see a big smile!" Cyndi called out in a playful voice that had only a slightly sharp edge.

Dutifully, they both smiled.

"Isn't that adorable!" the reporter whispered to the photographer.

"Oh, yeah," he grunted, rolling his eyes. "Adorable." Still, he raised his camera and took a few quick photos.

Cyndi moved closer to Miley and nudged her. "Go ahead," she said in a low, steely voice. "Say something else."

Miley cleared her throat, searching her mind for a few witty—or even coherent—words. "So! You surf!" she said finally.

As soon as the words were out of her mouth, Miley wished she could call them back. Was there anyone else in the entire world who sounded more inane than her?

"Uh-huh," Talen said. "And you sing, right?"

Yes, apparently there was, and that person's name was Talen.

But Miley didn't have time to comfort herself with this fact, because just then she heard Cyndi whisper to the reporter, "Aren't they darling together?" The photographer's camera flashed a few more times, and she had to clench her hands into fists to resist the temptation to grab it and throw it into the sea.

She turned her attention back to Talen, who was holding something out to her and looking abashed.

It was an eight-by-ten color photo. Of her. Hannah Montana.

"I was wondering"—he had clearly given up on direct eye contact and was now speaking to the floor—"if maybe you'd sign this for me?"

"Talen," Cyndi triumphantly explained to everyone within earshot, "is Hannah's number one fan! Aren't you, Talen?"

Miley had to work hard to keep her jaw from dropping in complete and utter astonishment. Talen Wright was a fan . . . of Hannah Montana? Talen Wright was acting . . . starstruck?

But what about all that stuff he had said about not being into celebrities, about wanting to meet real people instead, about hating fame? Maybe Jessica was right about Talen, after all.

"Yeah," he mumbled. "I mean, I have all your CDs and everything. . . ." His voice trailed off. He took a deep breath. "Actually, I was wondering if I could ask you a question?"

"Well, sure!" she said, turning up the

wattage on her bright Hannah Montana smile. She wanted to cover up how uncomfortable she was feeling.

"How did you find out you liked to sing?" he asked. "You never talk about that in any interviews."

She hesitated. "That's a good question." She paused to gather her thoughts, and the memory of that conversation at dawn flashed into her mind. "I think I've loved music from before I was born. And now, when I'm onstage, I feel at home. Like this is where I was born to be."

He gave her a startled look as if he heard an echo from that morning as well. "That's exactly how I feel about surfing."

"That's an important thing, isn't it, to know what you're meant to be doing?" she said. "And who you should be doing it with."

"Yeah," he said slowly. "I think you're right."

Their eyes met. And, for the briefest of

moments, she felt that true connection again, the one they had when he knew her as ordinary, everyday Miley Stewart.

Then the camera flash went off once more and they both blinked in surprise. The spell was broken.

Later that night, Miley was lying on her bed, staring at the ceiling and wondering how the awesome summer she had planned had gotten so complicated.

After the incredibly awkward meeting with Talen, she and Lilly had gotten into the car. As her dad drove to Lilly's house to drop her off, Lilly couldn't stop talking about what had just happened.

"Wow, Miley, Talen is *so* into you!" she kept saying.

"Not *me*," Miley kept pointing out. "Hannah Montana."

Lilly looked puzzled. "Miley, you *are* Hannah Montana."

"I know that!" Miley had snapped. "But *Talen* doesn't!"

Frustrated, she crossed her arms and looked out the car window, only to see her own reflection—her blond-wigged, fully made up, glam-clothes-wearing Hannah Montana reflection—staring back at her. She stuck out her tongue at her pop singer persona and turned back to Lilly. "I can't believe he likes some other girl better than me! And I can't believe that the other girl he likes better than me is actually *me!*"

"Okay, I admit it." Lilly pulled off her wig and fluffed out her hair. "This *is* a weird situation. Not one you run into every day."

"No kidding," Miley groaned. "This is so confusing."

"But look on the bright side!" Lilly added as they pulled up in front of her house, "No matter who Talen ends up liking, you still win!"

"Ya think?" Miley muttered, but Lilly was already getting out of the car and didn't hear.

After Miley and her dad got home, he cooked her favorite meal—meat loaf and mashed potatoes—but she barely tasted it. She tried watching TV, but none of the shows seemed interesting. She considered teasing Jackson about his brand-new sunburn, but she didn't have the heart.

Finally she trudged up the stairs to her bedroom. She stretched out on her bed and stared out the window. The moon, surrounded by hundreds of glittering stars, hung low in the velvet black sky.

A perfect night for a romantic walk on the beach, Miley thought. Assuming, that is, that the boy you had started to really, really like hadn't become a complete and utter mystery.

Then she heard a knock on the door, and her dad poked his head in.

"You seemed lower than a snake on a dirt road at supper," he said. "Want to tell me what's wrong?"

"Oh . . . nothing," Miley said.

He came in and sat on a chair by her bed. "It didn't look like nothing when you refused second helpings of my special cheesy mashed potatoes," he said. "And I even used chives to give it that extra little kick."

"Sorry, Daddy," she said softly. "They were good. Really."

"Well, thanks, honey. That was real convincing." He leaned forward to look her in the eye. "Come on, bud. What's wrong?"

"Oh . . . *everything.*"

"So we've gone from nothing being wrong to everything being wrong." He nodded. "That's progress, I guess."

She grinned faintly, but then her smile slipped away. "It's Talen," she said. "I thought he was so cool and then it turns out that he's just as starstruck as anybody else! He was falling all over me after rehearsal, and he doesn't even know anything about Hannah Montana except what he's read in magazines! Everything he told me feels like a lie!"

Mr. Stewart sighed and put his arm around her shoulders. "This is exactly why we wanted to set it up so you could have a normal life," her dad said. "The older you get, the more successful you get, you'll start meeting people who want to be your friends, and you'll always be wondering: do they like me for me? Or because I'm famous? Talen may be a secret Hannah Montana fan, but I have a feeling he also really likes Miley Stewart."

"You think?" she asked wistfully.

"No," he said.

She twisted around to look into his eyes, hurt.

"I don't *think* he likes Miley," her dad said. "I know it for a fact. And if I were you, I'd give the boy a chance. He has a lot of weight on his shoulders, too."

Miley rolled her eyes—her dad could be so corny!—but she was smiling. "Okay," she said. As he got up to leave, she added, "Thanks, Dad."

"Any time, bud." He winked and closed the door behind him.

She flopped onto her back, replaying her father's words in her mind. After a while, she began to sense words and images floating to the surface of her mind. She leaned over to grab her guitar and began strumming it thoughtfully, her head tilted to one side as she tried to catch the lyrics that still seemed to dance in the air, just out of her reach.

"Living the life, living the dream," she murmured. She played a few more chords, thinking. "Everything's perfect, or so it would seem. . . ."

She stopped strumming and sighed.

Talen had seemed so perfect. So real. And now it turned out he wasn't. Did that mean she couldn't be his friend? Or did that just make him human? She felt so confused.

Somehow, Miley knew, turning her sadness into a song would make her feel . . . well, not happier, exactly, but better somehow. Stronger. Calmer. Peaceful.

"Still a soul surfer, you go your own way,"

she sang softly. "Or is that just something it sounds good to say?"

Outside, the moon slowly rose and turned the surf to silver, while in her bedroom Miley kept singing.

From Miley Stewart's Journal

After my dad encouraged my songwriting, I threw myself into my music. That was all I thought about, day in and day out. I used to get in trouble in school sometimes, because teachers thought I was daydreaming. I wanted to explain that I was actually working, because I was making up lyrics in my mind, but I knew enough to realize that this would not go over well when the class I was taking was geography or algebra!

Finally, my dad realized how serious I was. That's when he decided to put my passion to the test. One Saturday afternoon, he took me down to a music hall in Nashville. It wasn't open yet, because it was only about two o'clock, but the owner let us in to talk to a friend of my dad's.

His name was Junebug Johnson (I

don't think Junebug was the name his parents gave him, but whatever they named him must have been pretty awful, because it was a deep, dark secret.) He was about sixty years old, wearing a red checked shirt, old jeans with suspenders, and cracked brown leather shoes. He was completely bald, but he had white whiskers. He looked a lot like Santa Claus would look if he had been born and raised on a farm in Tennessee.

He was sitting at a little table, tuning his guitar. My dad and I sat down with him. Then Junebug and my dad talked for a long time about music. I could tell my dad thought Junebug was a great player. After a while he pulled out his own guitar and played a few songs he had written and asked for Junebug's advice. Junebug made some comments that sounded pretty smart to me.

Then Junebug started playing, and I couldn't believe my ears. I'd never heard anyone play like that. Every note rang true and clear; every chord seemed to make the air shiver with emotion. And his voice . . . it was deep and rich and filled with light and shadows. It made me think of the creek behind our house, the way it danced over rocks in the shallow part and glided along, silent and mysterious, where it ran deep. The place had paint peeling off the walls, there were only a dozen tables on the splintery floor, and the posters tacked up around the room were faded and curling at the edges. But listening to Junebug Johnson sing was the best concert I've ever been to in my life.

After about an hour, Junebug had to stop playing for us so he could get ready for his gig that night. Before we left, though, my dad said to Junebug, "Miley here thinks she might want to be in the music business someday."

"That right?" Junebug looked at me

over the top of his glasses. I remember that look so clearly. It was very focused, as if he were trying to see into my soul. "You like music?"

"Yes, sir, I do." I hesitated, then I told the truth. "I love it."

My dad met Junebug's eyes. "She's good," he said. "She could be really good."

"Hmmph." Junebug didn't say anything for a long time. Then he sighed and said, "Well, if you really love music, there's nothing better than spending your life singing and playing. But that's got to be enough for you, you understand?"

I nodded, but he gave me another one of those looks, so I told the truth again. "No, not really."

"Well now, you take a look at me," he said. "I've always loved music, too, but I never got my big break. I never got famous. I never made a lot of money." He stopped and stared right into my eyes. "But I've lived my life doing what I have a passion for, even though most of the time I'm playing in places like this to maybe ten people. And nine of those people just came in to get out of the rain. But I don't care, because that one person who came for the music, that's the person I'm playing for. And that's enough for me."

Chapter Thirteen

Are you everything you seem?
Or are you just a summer dream?

"Well, Talen, looks like you're kind of into celebrities after all," Jessica said in a snide voice. Her words echoed the thoughts that had been running through Miley's head since the night before. Throwing a copy of *Entertainment Insider* onto Talen's desk, Jessica smiled slyly. Even from across the aisle, Miley could see the headline: EXCLUSIVE! HANNAH + TALEN! A MATCH MADE IN MALIBU!

There was a photo, too, from the rehearsal. Somehow the photographer had managed to catch a moment when Hannah and Talen had both been smiling at the same time. If tabloid readers didn't look too closely, it might even look as if they were smiling at each other.

Miley suppressed a groan. She had to force herself to look over at Talen, sure that he would be frowning at the sight of that ridicculous photo, that sensational headline, the sheer cheesiness of it all. . . .

But Talen, much to her surprise, had a slight smile on his face. In fact, if it wasn't Talen, surfing champion and all-around cool guy, Miley would have said that he even looked a little . . . goofy.

"All right, class, let's get started," Mr. Dickson said. "This is our last day together—"

He was interrupted by a small cheer from the back row, where Dan, Eugene, and Jackie were sitting.

Mr. Dickson glared at them. "So let's try to end on a high point. Now, I have your journals to return to you—"

Before he could go on, Stefan grabbed the magazine for a closer look. "Dude!" he cried.

"When did you start hanging out with Hannah Montana?"

Talen shrugged, but he looked pleased. "Oh, we've been tight for a while," he said.

"What?" Jessica said sharply. "Since when?"

"Since . . . I don't know . . . a while ago," he said, shrugging.

"And what do you mean, you're tight?" Jessica asked dangerously. "I repeat, since when?"

Good questions, Miley thought. I can't wait to hear the answer.

"You know, we hang out," he said, not meeting Jessica's eyes. "We've been hanging out for a while."

"That's awesome!" Even Dan Barton, the slacker prince of Seaview High School, looked impressed by this.

In fact, everyone in the class was listening with interest. Mr. Dickson had even stopped in the aisle in order to hear what Talen had to say about Hannah Montana.

"So, what's she really like, Talen?" Stefan asked. "Total diva, right?"

Miley shot him an irritated look. Typical! Just because she was an international pop star, people had to assume she was superdemanding! When the truth was—

"Oh, no, she's really cool," Talen said. When this didn't seem to satisfy his audience, he went on. "She really likes to, um, go in-line skating. And, er, sing karaoke. Although, of course, she totally blows everyone away when she sings. Her favorite color is red, she loves horror movies . . ."

Miley's mouth dropped open. Where was he getting this stuff? She hated in-line skating. Horror movies gave her nightmares. And even though she performed onstage as Hannah Montana, she was too nervous to try karaoke as Miley Stewart.

". . . and she's so funny!" Talen went on. "Great sense of humor."

Well, Miley thought, that was kind of sweet

of him. . . . Then she caught herself. What was she thinking? He had no idea whether Hannah Montana was funny enough to be a stand-up comic or serious as a stick! He was making everything up!

"So," Miley said innocently, "how did you two meet?"

"Well, it turns out she heard about me during the Breakpoint Surf Series coverage on ESPN," he said airily.

"Really?" Miley asked. "Hannah Montana follows the tour results?"

"Oh, yeah." he nodded. "She's a big, big surfing fan. Huge. So she had her manager get in touch with me."

Jessica gave a disdainful sniff. "She wasn't brave enough to call you herself?"

"No, she's actually very shy," Talen snapped. He gave Jessica a meaningful look. "Which *I* think is sweet."

"Sweet!" Jessica muttered. "More like insipid."

"I mean, for such a big star, she doesn't put on airs at all," he continued. "She's completely down-to-earth."

Huh, Miley thought. And exactly how would you know that, Mr. Gotta-Keep-It-Real? From the in-depth coverage about her in *Entertainment Insider*?

Before she had the chance to say that aloud, Mr. Dickson cleared his throat. "While it's been fascinating getting the inside scoop on Hannah Montana, we do need to get down to business."

The teacher started down the aisle again, dropping off journals on the students' desks. "Very good work, everyone. I really enjoyed reading all your journal entries." He handed Miley her notebook. "Trying your hand at song lyrics was very inventive, Miley. You might want to look into music as a possible career someday. You seem to have a real feel for it."

"Thanks, Mr. Dickson," Miley said as she

flipped her notebook open. On the last page was a big red A. "Maybe I will."

From his seat across the aisle, Talen shot her his first sincere smile of the day, as though everything were fine and he hadn't just completely shattered her illusions about him. When she didn't return it, Talen cocked his head. "You okay?" he asked quietly.

"Shouldn't you be asking yourself that question?" Miley said. Her voice was cool. "What happened to hating celebrities and the fame game? I mean, all that stuff you wrote in your journal! And that day we went surfing, you said—"

Her voice trembled and she bit her lip. She didn't want him to think she was about to cry. She didn't want him to think she cared that much.

"Just forget it."

Talen blinked in surprise. "Miley, listen—" he began.

But Miley was too confused and hurt to

hear any excuses from Talen. "I thought better of you. I thought you were real."

And with that, she looked back down at her journal and didn't speak to him for the rest of the class.

Chapter Fourteen

Let's rock, let's roll, let's go, okay!
Don't let anything stand in your way

Oliver stared out to sea, his eyes inscrutable behind dark sunglasses, one arm casually hooked around his surfboard. Although he did his best to look as if he were unaware of anyone around him, he was actually darting quick little sideways glances at people passing by, hoping that they were impressed by the new, improved, and completely hip Oliver Oken.

Jackson stood beside him, striking a similar nonchalant pose. "Check it out," he said out of the side of his mouth. "Those girls from the other day . . ."

Oliver squinted. Sure enough, Pamela,

Annie, and—his heart skipped a beat—
Daphne had just joined a few other surfers at
the edge of the water. They were talking and
laughing with a redheaded guy that Oliver
remembered seeing with Talen—Stefan, that
was it—and a girl who also looked vaguely
familiar. Long blond hair, streaked a bunch of
different colors . . . Oh, right. Oliver rolled his
eyes. Lilly's new best friend, Jessica.

At that moment he saw Lilly run out of the
water to greet Jessica and Stefan. They stood
some distance away, talking animatedly and
watching other surfers as they paddled out and
caught the waves that were rolling into shore
with thunderous regularity.

Oliver watched them from a distance and
scowled. Lilly had promised she would go out
to get ice cream with him the night before,
then she never showed up. She didn't even call
to make an excuse or say she was sorry.

"I can't believe Lilly didn't call me," he
grumbled. "I happen to know I'm number

three on her speed dial. Number one are her parents, number two is Miley, and number three is me. One button, that's all she had to push, and I wouldn't have spent hours playing pinochle with my mom—"

"Dude, cut it out," Jackson muttered. "Remember rule number forty-three."

"Whining isn't cool," Oliver muttered back reluctantly. Jackson had sprung that rule on him half an hour ago, after Oliver had vented one too many times about how much he'd been looking forward to that scoop of mint chocolate chip. And how completely boring pinochle was.

"Exactly." Beside him, Jackson was sucking in his stomach, sticking his chest out, and crossing his arms strategically to make it look as if he had biceps. He was squinting at the distant horizon, looking calm, confident, and completely cool. . . .

Until, that is, Stefan called out, "Hey, dude. Awesome surfboard."

Startled, Jackson whipped his head around, dislodging his sunglasses, which fell to the sand. He tried to grab them while still holding his surfboard, lost his balance, and pitched forward face-first onto the beach. His board landed on top of him, bonking him on the head.

Oliver winced. He knew only too well how embarrassing it was to fall flat on your face. Especially when all you were doing was standing still.

But Jackson jumped to his feet, looking completely unabashed. "Thanks, man," he said, trying to brush sand out of his hair. "It's pretty beat up, but then, it's seen a lot of action."

Before training with Jackson, Oliver wouldn't have thought such an outrageous statement would be taken seriously. But Stefan nodded respectfully, and Pamela and Annie, who had wandered over, actually looked impressed.

Daphne, however, gave Oliver a little wink,

as if they shared a secret. Surprised, he grinned back at her.

"The surf looks killer," Jackson added.

"No lie," Pamela said. "Have you been in yet?"

"Oh, uh, no, not yet," Jackson said evasively. "We just got here a few minutes ago. Had some things to take care of earlier today."

Oliver noted with envy how Jackson managed to invest these words with deep meaning, as if he'd had some mysterious and vitally important errand to perform—saving the planet from imminent doom, perhaps, or exposing an international spy ring—rather than eating cereal out of the box while watching afternoon television.

"Yeah, me, too," Stefan said. "Jessica and I were being held prisoner in a summer-school class! Right in the middle of the tour, too."

"That's too bad," Oliver agreed. Jackson shot him a glance and he hastily corrected himself. "I mean, um, bummer, man!"

"Yeah, I've been bleak," Stefan said. "But today was the last day, so life is good. So. You guys ready to hit the waves?"

Jackson's normally cheerful expression faded. He looked pale. "I'd love to, but—"

"C'mon, don't book out on us again!" Stefan said. "The surf's awesome today."

"I've got to go to work in ten minutes," Oliver said quickly. "Otherwise, I'd be right there with you. For sure."

"Bummer about the job," Stefan said. "I know what it's like to need bucks."

As Oliver sighed with relief, Stefan turned to Jackson. "But, dude, you *gotta* get out there! Those are the best waves I've seen all week."

"Yeah, come on, Jackson," Pamela said. She winked flirtatiously at him. "We'll have fun."

Oliver sneaked a quick peek at Jackson, who looked too stunned to speak. His mouth was opening and closing, but no words were coming out. He looked, Oliver couldn't help but think, the exact opposite of cool.

"Yeah, brah," Stefan said, giving Jackson a friendly little shove toward the ocean. "You've been talking about how you can't wait to rip those waves! Now's your chance to show your stuff!"

"Right," Jackson said, shooting Oliver a desperate look. He started moving toward the water with the slow, measured gait of a man walking to his doom. "Now's my chance."

Even from the safety of the beach, Jackson's attempt at surfing looked disastrous. Oliver shuddered to think what it was like for him out there battling the waves.

First, he lost his grip on his surfboard before he even got past the break and had to flail around in the water to get it back. Then he gripped it tightly, dived under the breakwater, and came up coughing so badly that Pamela had to paddle over and make sure he could still breathe. Then he misjudged the first wave's approach, paddled out too late, and was spun around without even getting up on his board. Pamela called out something to him, clearly giving him advice, and it seemed to work. At least Jackson managed to stand on his board for the second wave, but then he promptly tumbled off. The third wave smashed over his head; he popped to the surface, sputtering. The fourth wave—

But at that point, Oliver had to turn away. Some things were just too painful to watch.

"It's just not his day, is it?" Daphne said sympathetically.

"Guess not," Oliver said. There was a brief silence as he tried to think of something else to say. Miraculously, the third principle for talking to girls came to mind, and he blurted out, "I like your . . . um . . . rash guard."

"You do?" Surprised, Daphne looked down at the completely ordinary white rash guard she was wearing. "Well, thanks."

"Sure." There was another silence, longer this time.

Just when Oliver thought it would last forever, they were interrupted. He was glad for the interruption, but not for what caused it.

"Hi, Oliver! Hi, Daphne!" Lilly called out cheerfully as she and Jessica strolled up.

"Lilly," Oliver said, making his voice distant and cold.

"Did you guys see my last set?" she asked eagerly.

"Yeah, you looked awesome," Daphne said. "You were really ripping that wave."

"Yes, Lilly's surfing is *so* much better than it was a few days ago," Jessica interrupted. Somehow, Oliver thought, this didn't actually sound very nice, the way Jessica said it.

Then she turned to Lilly and added kindly, "You almost stalled out, though. If you do that in competition, your scores will drop like a rock."

Out of the corner of his eye, Oliver saw Daphne roll her eyes ever so slightly.

Lilly's face fell. "Okay. I'll try to remember that," she said.

Oliver couldn't help it; he felt a little sorry for Lilly. She was usually so confident. And now Jessica was making her sound unsure of herself and . . . *small*, somehow.

"You looked great to me," he blurted out. "Fantastic! Awesome!"

It wasn't cool; it wasn't laid-back; it wasn't in accordance with any of Jackson's rules.

But it seemed like the right thing to say.

Daphne beamed at him. Lilly cast a grateful glance his way.

"Thanks," she said.

"Not that you actually *know* anything about surfing," Jessica pointed out. She grabbed her surfboard. "Come on, Lilly. I need more practice. And so do you."

Lilly looked from Jessica to Oliver, then back to Jessica. Lilly's chin lifted one inch, in a way that Oliver was quite familiar with. It meant she was digging her heels in, determined to do things her own way.

"I'll be there in a minute," Lilly said.

"If you don't want to embarrass yourself tomorrow, you'll need every minute you can get on the waves today," Jessica said.

Lilly gave her a level look. "I *said* I'll be there in a minute."

"Fine," Jessica said. "What*ever*."

As she walked off in a huff, Lilly muttered, "And I won't embarrass myself tomorrow, either."

When he was sure Jessica was out of earshot, Oliver said, "That was great, Lilly, the way you stood up to her. Remind me to call you if I'm ever threatened by a street gang. Or even a mean crossing guard."

As jokes went, he had to admit it wasn't his best. But Lilly didn't even chuckle. Instead, she looked at him with such a tragic expression that he was somewhat alarmed.

"What? I'm paying you a compliment," he explained.

Lilly didn't seem to hear him. "Listen, Oliver," she blurted out. "I'm sorry I didn't call you last night. I know you're mad at me, and you have every right to be."

Oliver furrowed his brow in momentary confusion. Then he remembered. Oh, that's right. He *was* mad at Lilly.

"And I'm sorry we haven't been hanging out," she went on earnestly. "I just got so caught up in the surfing competition, but I swear I'll make it up to you—"

"That's okay," he said. Now that she was apologizing with such sincerity, he couldn't quite recall why it had seemed like such a big deal.

"No, really," Lilly insisted. "I feel sooooo bad, and so I thought—"

"Really, it's okay," he said, faintly irritated. Why was Lilly going on about this, especially in front of Daphne?

Lilly leaned in and stared meaningfully into his eyes. Oliver went on alert. He knew that stare. It was a stare that meant, Shut up and pay attention, Oliver! So he did.

"As I was saying," she went on, clipping off each word, "I thought I'd buy you a smoothie. But then I remembered that your job is making smoothies! Which I happened to mention to Daphne and, as it turns out, she adores smoothies!"

Oliver gulped. "You do?" he asked Daphne.

"Oh, yes," she said, her eyes sparkling. "Absolutely."

"So I told her how you make the best smoothies in Malibu, and she said she'd love to try one," Lilly said. "So I thought maybe you and Daphne could go to Rico's sometime?"

"What a great idea!" Daphne said in a voice that didn't sound altogether real. "In fact"— she made a surprised face, as if a thought had just struck her—"how about right now?"

"Sure," he said faintly, with the feeling that he was in the grip of a force far larger than himself.

"Cool!" Daphne said. "Let me just grab my

bag and I'll be right with you!"

She ran over to where she had left her towel and beach bag. As soon as she was out of earshot, Lilly grinned at Oliver. "I guess I'll have to make it up to you some other time," she said, her voice back to normal.

"Thanks." He grinned back at her. "I think you already have."

Chapter Fifteen

Where we're going I don't know
So ride the wave and just let go!

The morning of the Breakpoint Surf Series dawned bright and clear. Miley, Jackson, Oliver, and Mr. Stewart joined the crowd at the beach to watch the first heats for the novice division.

"And in the first heat, Lilly Truscott and Liz Rudd!" The announcer's voice boomed out over the PA system.

They all cheered as Lilly picked a perfect wave and rode it to shore. Then they cheered again when her scores went up and she advanced to the next round.

She competed in two more rounds before wiping out and being knocked out of the competition. But when she ran up to them, her hair slicked back and dripping with salt-water, she was beaming.

"That was so cool!" she cried.

"*You* are so cool!" Miley corrected her.

"Great job, Lilly," Mr. Stewart said as Jackson and Oliver gave her high fives.

For the next hour, they all watched as pairs of novice and intermediate surfers competed in one heat after another. Daphne and Annie went all the way to the finals, but Pamela was knocked out in the semifinal round. She ran out of the surf, shrugging good-naturedly as spectators called out, "Better luck next time!" and "Great effort!"

Pamela looked around, scanning the crowd. When she saw Jackson and Oliver, she grinned and ran over the sand to where they were standing.

"Hey, guys!"

"Hi," Oliver said happily. He liked Pamela. She was nice. And she was a friend of

Daphne's. And after yesterday afternoon, when he had made a smoothie for Daphne and then talked to her for three hours straight, he was filled with warmth and goodwill toward everyone on the planet.

Jackson, however, looked uncomfortable. He wouldn't meet Pamela's eyes. "Hey. Good heat," he muttered.

"It was terrible," she said cheerfully. "But who cares, right? That's the great thing about surfing, there's always another wave."

"I guess so." Jackson shrugged, his eyes glued to the sand.

Oliver gave him an exasperated look. Where was the cool, devil-may-care Jackson who had lectured him about ruling the beach with attitude and moxie? And who was this glum imposter who had taken his place? Was he embarrassed by yesterday's wipeouts?

Oliver had just about decided it was time to intervene on his friend's behalf when Pamela nudged Jackson with her elbow. "Hey, I wanted to tell you how impressive you were on the waves yesterday," she said.

"Yeah, right," Jackson said, but he risked a quick glance at her.

"No, really," she said. "You showed a lot of guts, the way you kept trying, no matter what."

Jackson perked up a bit at that. "Well, it wasn't my best day, for sure. But like you said, there's always another wave."

Her eyes gleamed with humor. "Exactly. And you know"—she leaned in conspiratorially—"I hang out with surfer dudes all day long. It's kind of refreshing to meet a guy who thinks about something besides the breakpoint."

"Yeah?" Jackson's face filled with hope.

"Yeah." Pamela nodded. "Hey, want to go get a smoothie?"

"Sure," Jackson said. He puffed out his chest a little bit, looking more like the Jackson that Oliver was used to seeing. "I actually make the best smoothie on the beach, you know."

"I think I heard that somewhere," she said.

"So let me show you." As he led Pamela down the beach, Oliver heard him say, "I'll even throw in some mango. . . ."

When it was time for Talen's first heat, Miley could sense the extra electricity in the air. Not only was he a popular surfer, he was battling Grady O'Shea for first place in the series' standings. As Talen sat on his surfboard, waiting to choose his wave, the crowd noise got even louder.

Miley watched Talen, who looked very small and alone in the vast expanse of ocean, and thought back to that perfect morning when they had watched the sun rise together and she had ridden her first wave. The contrast between that peaceful time and now—with hundreds of people shouting and cheering, music playing at a deafening level, loudspeakers blaring out announcements and scores, and helicopters circling overhead—couldn't have been more dramatic.

I wonder what's going through his mind right now, Miley thought as she watched a wave approach. I wonder what he's feeling. . . . She expected Talen to take that wave, to jump up and ride it with total command, complete control.

But he didn't. Instead, Grady O'Shea grabbed the opportunity and turned in a spectacular ride, ending with a celebratory flip off his board.

The crowd cheered for Grady, of course. But Miley could see people near her exchange puzzled glances, then turn back to wait for Talen to make his move.

I wonder if he's remembering that morning, too, Miley thought, as another wave drew near. Once again, Talen hesitated, then let it pass.

"What's wrong with him?" Lilly muttered in her ear.

Miley shook her head. "I don't know."

Lilly looked at her out of the corner of her eye. "Maybe he's not thinking about surfing," she suggested.

"What else would he be thinking about?" Miley asked, trying to sound indifferent. She squinted against the sun and watched as a perfect wave rose up on the horizon and began moving toward shore. The crowd stirred with excitement.

"That's the best wave of the day!" Lilly said. "He's *got* to take that one. He'll rack up an incredible score—"

But when the wave rolled into shore, Talen was still sitting on his surfboard, staring at the horizon.

"Come *on*," Lilly said impatiently. "What is he doing?"

The buzzer sounded, ending the heat. A murmur of disappointment ran through the crowd. Talen had lost his chance, and the competition.

Even from the beach, Miley could see him shake his head. Then he shrugged and began paddling back in.

Miley and Lilly glanced at each other.

"Wow," Lilly said.

"Yeah," Miley said.

Miley watched Talen pick up his board and trudge across the beach, his head down. Her last words to Talen ran through her mind. *I thought better of you. I thought you were real.*

She bit her lip. Had Talen been hearing those words, too, as he sat on his surfboard and watched one wave after another pass him by?

Chapter Sixteen

Trust your heart, take a chance, find a way
Anything can happen on a summer day

A few hours later, Miley stood backstage and peeked out at the crowd that had gathered on the beach in front of the stage. Then she whirled around and walked over to the small table and mirror that served as a temporary dressing table.

She peered nervously at her reflection and brushed on another layer of mascara.

"Stop it!" Lilly said. She was backstage, too, dressed as Lola Luftnagle. "You look great."

"Are you sure?" Miley checked herself out again. She was wearing a new Hannah Montana outfit, her blond wig, and full stage makeup.

"Yes!" Lilly said, exasperated. "I've told you twelve times already."

"Did the sound check go okay?" Miley asked. She ran back to the front of the stage to look through the curtain again. She could hear the low, excited hum of hundreds of voices getting ready for the concert to begin. "And the band—how were they?"

"Everything sounded awesome," Lilly reassured her. "Why are you so jumpy? You've done this show a million times."

"I know, I know." Miley bit her lip. "But this concert is different. . . ."

"Uh-huh." Lilly gave her a knowing look. "I think you mean the *audience* is different."

"What are you talking about?" Miley tried to sound innocent, but she could tell from the expression on Lilly's face that her friend wasn't buying it.

"Come on, Miley. I don't have to be a mind reader to tell what you're thinking about," Lilly said. "It's like you have a neon light over your head, flashing 'Talen, Talen, Talen!'"

Miley blushed. "Okay, maybe I am thinking about him. I mean, maybe a little bit. But we haven't talked since he was all ga-ga over that picture of us—I mean him and Hannah. He did try to explain himself, but I wasn't in the mood to listen." She gave Lilly a miserable look. "And now I don't know whether I should be mad at him or hear him out."

"I get that you're disappointed in him," Lilly said slowly. She hesitated. "But it *is* kind of cool that he's such a Hannah Montana fan. . . ."

"Okay! Yes, you're right! Agreed! And I may have been overly harsh!" Miley cried, her mood switching from miserable to anxious. "But that's another thing! What if he doesn't like my performance? What if I do something stupid, like trip over an electrical cord or fall off the stage? What if I suddenly lose my voice? What if—"

"What if you lose your mind and start worrying about imaginary disasters?" Lilly interrupted. "Oh, wait, that already happened." She snapped her fingers in front of Miley's nose. "Snap out of it! You can figure out the Talen situation later. For now, just take a few deep breaths and remember all the times you've done this show perfectly. You'll be fine."

Miley took two deep breaths, as instructed, and felt a sense of calm fill her body. She smiled at her friend. "Hey, you're right."

"What a surprise," Lilly said smugly.

And Lilly *was* right. Miley hit the stage with energy and started singing. By the end of the first song, she knew she was in the groove. The crowd responded with cheers and applause, and she felt the familiar and completely wonderful sensation of being carried along by their enthusiasm.

The whole time she was performing, however, her eyes were scanning the audience. It was somewhere in the middle of the second song—around the time she was hitting the chorus for the first time—that she spotted him.

Talen was sitting in the fifth row center. He was bobbing his head to the music, smiling. Miley relaxed.

At least he looks like he's enjoying himself, she thought.

Then she had to forget about everything except her performance. In fact, she couldn't even look in Talen's direction again; he was just too distracting.

By the time the concert was almost over, Miley was riding a wave of adrenaline, totally in her element, feeling free and happy. As she finished the second to the last song, however, she felt a quiver of nerves in her stomach.

Now was the moment. As she waited for the audience to stop clapping, she felt her knees tremble. The applause finally died down enough for her to step forward to the microphone.

"Thank you so much," she said. "Y'all have

been a great audience. Now, before we wrap it up, I'd like to try something a little different. . . ."

A few minutes later, Miley was sitting on a stool and holding her acoustic guitar in a tight grip. Her heart was pounding; she took a deep breath to steady it. As Hannah Montana, Miley usually performed with a band. She rarely sang in front of an audience the way she did at home: simple, direct, just her and a guitar and her own honest emotions.

She was thankful at this moment that she was holding her own guitar, one her dad had given her when she had started writing songs. It fit her hands and her body with comforting familiarity.

She gazed out at the audience. It looked like a huge, faceless mass, and she felt her stomach turn over again. Was she crazy to do what she was about to do?

Then she seemed to hear the voice of her dad's friend, Junebug Johnson, telling her about a trick he used for years to overcome stage fright.

"Find one friendly face," he had said. "Sing to that person, not the whole crowd. You'll forget all the other people and stop feeling so afraid. And sometimes, if all the stars line up just perfect, you'll touch that person"—he tapped on his chest—"right here in the heart."

Her eyes searched for Talen in the crowd. Darkness had fallen, but she could see his blond hair shining silver in the light of the moon.

"So . . . this is a new song I just wrote," Miley announced, her voice quavering slightly. She had spent hours reworking the lyrics she had scribbled in her journal over the last two weeks, tightening and cutting and rearranging them until they were, she hoped, just right. "It's very personal and so I . . . I hope you like it." She strummed the opening chords and sang:

First I saw his laughing eyes
Blue as the sea, blue as the skies.

Hit me like a wave that summer day
Told me come along and play.

You took my hand and said let's go,
I'll teach you a whole new show.
Feel the waves and catch a few.
Will you catch me? Will I catch you?

Even from a distance, she could see Talen tilt his head, looking suddenly interested. She swung into the chorus. She had tried to capture the spirit of summer in the words, and even as she sang them, dozens of memories of the last two weeks ran through her mind:

Ride the wave—
Summer sun, summer fun, summer love.
Ride the wave—
Let it bring you what you're dreaming of.
Ride the wave—
Let's rock, let's roll, let's go, okay!
Anything can happen on a summer day.

She could sense people starting to move to the music as the hook caught them. The sense of excitement and fun continued through the next verse:

No time to think, no time to fear
Now it's time to take the dare.
I'm standing tall, I'm flying free
Now I've found a whole new me.

Then her voice became more introspective, more questioning:

Falling under, lost in the tide,
But there you are, right by my side.
In your heart you feel the sea
Ride the waves and you feel free.

Talen sat forward on his seat, his expression bemused.

After singing the chorus again, she

launched into the last two verses, trying to put everything she felt, everything she had been thinking about Talen, into the words:

> Play it cool, that's your style
> What's behind the secret smile?
> Soul surfer, you go you own way
> Or is that just something it sounds good
>   to say?

> Are you everything you seem?
> Or are you just a summer dream?
> Where we're going I don't know,
> So ride the wave and just let go!

By the time she got to the last chorus, the audience was singing along.

> Ride the wave—
> Summer sun, summer fun, summer love.
> Ride the wave—
> Let it bring you what you're dreaming of.

Ride the wave—
Trust your heart, take a chance, find a way,
Anything can happen on a summer day.

For a few seconds after Miley finished the song, there was a hushed silence. Miley felt a stab of fear. Oh, no, she thought. They hated it! I looked like an idiot! Why did I think this was a good idea. . . .

Then the audience erupted into cheers.

But Miley didn't hear or see anything except Talen, who was smiling as if her song had just touched him. Right in the heart.

After her last big number, Miley ran backstage to be congratulated by the band and crew.

"You did a great job, bud," her dad said, grinning and giving her a high five. "I think we're going to have to work 'Ride the Wave' into every show from now on."

"Yes, it was fantastic!" Cyndi came swooping

up, dragging along a sheepish Talen. "And look who I have here!"

"Hey." He nodded at Miley.

"I think it's someone who wants to tell you how much he enjoyed the concert!" Cyndi added in a singsong voice.

Talen looked utterly mortified.

"Let's walk over there," Miley suggested, nodding toward a backstage area that was relatively empty—and as far away from Cyndi as possible.

"Great idea," he said.

"I caught part of the competition today," Miley said once they had moved away. "I'm sorry things didn't go your way."

"Thanks," he said. He had a strange expression on his face, half puzzled, half amused. "That was kind of weird, actually. I've never been so . . . unsure of myself in a competition."

"What was going on?" Miley asked. She held her breath, waiting for the answer.

He shrugged one shoulder. "I don't know. I paddled out, I was good to go . . . and then, all of a sudden, I saw a bird fly across the sky. I never notice things like that in the middle of a heat; I'm always totally focused. But once I saw the bird, I started noticing the way the clouds looked, and the feeling of the ocean swells, and the smell of the ocean air, and . . . I just didn't care about winning a trophy anymore. I just wanted to enjoy the moment."

Miley smiled gently. That's the Talen I met on the first day of summer school, she thought. That's the Talen I want to know.

But out loud, she just said, "Trophies have to be polished too much anyway."

"Yeah, tarnish is a major bummer," he agreed, grinning. "Anyway, I'm glad the night ended with your concert. I really liked it."

"Thanks," Miley said. "Um . . . any part in particular?"

"Well, yeah." He glanced around to make

sure no one had moved within earshot, then leaned forward. "That new song? The acoustic one? Where did you get the idea for that?"

"Who knows where ideas come from?" Miley said lightly. "Sometimes I feel like songs are floating around in the air, just waiting for me to hear them and write them down."

"Oh. Yeah." For a moment, it looked as if he were going to accept this, then he took a deep breath. "But that song . . . I mean, it really spoke to me, y'know? It was like you were inside my head or something."

She smiled with genuine happiness. "Thanks! That's exactly what I hoped you— um, that is, people in the audience would say."

Before Talen could ask anything else, Cyndi rushed up to them. "Soooo," she said coyly. "You two seem to be getting along well! I thought I'd tell you that I've booked a table at an adorable restaurant on the beach if you two want to have some time together. . . ."

Talen looked into Miley's eyes. "I'd really

like to," he said sincerely.

"Oh, *excellent*—" Cyndi began.

"But, I have someplace else I need to go," he finished. "And something else I need to take care of. I'm sorry."

Out of the corner of her eye, Miley saw Cyndi's face fall.

"No worries," Miley said. She couldn't resist adding, "After all, it's always a good thing to know where you're supposed to be."

For a heartbeat, there was a glimmer of recognition in Talen's eyes as he heard an echo of what they had talked about while watching the sun rise over the ocean. Then it passed, and he smiled. "Yeah," he said. "That's something I just figured out. And there's a girl I need to tell."

"Really." Miley smiled to herself. "She sounds pretty special. What's her name?"

"Miley," Talen said eagerly. "And she is, she's awesome. In fact, after hearing your new song, I think you two have a lot in common.

You'd really like her if you met her."

"I'm sure I would," she said, her eyes gleaming with mischief. "When you see Miley, be sure to say hello for me."

"I will," Talen said, smiling. "Thanks." He turned to go, his footsteps light and eager.

"Trust your heart, take a chance, find a way," she sang softly to herself as he disappeared into the crowd. "Anything can happen on a summer day."

Then she ran to change back into Miley, the girl Talen thought was awesome.

Acknowledgments

Special thanks to Liz Rudnick, for her superb editing skills, her good cheer, and her invaluable surfing knowledge, and to Deb Barnes for her songwriting expertise and her helpful insights into a musician's world.